CHEERLEADERS®

#12

STAYING TOGETHER

DIANE HOH

SCHOLASTIC INC.
New York Toronto London Auckland Sydney

ISBN 0-590-33928-1

Copyright © 1985 by Diane Hoh. All rights reserved. Published by Scholastic Inc.

12 11 10 9 8 7 6 5 4 3 2 1   12   5 6 7 8 9/8 0/9

STAYING TOGETHER

CHEERLEADERS

CHAPTER

"Whew, that was some workout!" Walt Manners gasped, throwing a towel around his stocky shoulders as he ran off the floor of the Tarenton High School gym. Ardith Engborg, the Varsity Cheerleaders' short blonde coach, had just blown her whistle to signal an end to the practice session.

"I'll say!" Mary Ellen Kirkwood, the squad's captain, agreed, pushing her corn-silk blonde hair off her face. "Tonight my aches will have aches!"

"Stop complaining," Nancy Goldstein scolded mildly. "We needed the practice." She handed a megaphone to Angie Poletti. "Here, carry this. I haven't got the strength."

Angie laughed, shaking her head with its honey-blonde hair so like Mary Ellen's. Angie didn't have Mary Ellen's stunning good looks, but her smile could light up any room, even one as big as the gym.

"Olivia," Walt said, putting his arm around tiny Olivia Evans, "I think the megaphones weigh more than you do. We need to fatten you up with a little pizza."

"Oh, boy," Angie groaned. "What I wouldn't give to hear someone say that to *me*!"

"That'll be the day," Preston Tilford III said, grinning, his dark blond hair slicked down with perspiration. He shook his handsome head. "That last side thigh stand with you almost buckled my knees."

Angie punched him in the arm, but she wasn't really mad. Everyone knew she was locked into a lifelong wrestling match with calories. Pizza and anything even faintly resembling chocolate were her worst enemies.

Olivia made a face at Walt. Years of medical care followed by years of hard work on her part had turned Olivia Evans from an invalid as a child to a healthy, athletic bundle of energy. Remarks about her slight frame rubbed her the wrong way. If it had been anyone but her adored Walt making the comment, she would have responded with an acid-laden reply.

Instead, she smiled up at Walt and quipped, "Every time we go for pizza you eat five slices in the time it takes me to eat one! No wonder I'm wasting away to nothing!"

Ardith, still in white shorts and top, reminded

all of them about the game with Deep River in two days.

"Stay limber!" she warned. "And avoid pizza at all costs!"

They all laughed and, picking up their towels, headed for the locker rooms.

Ben Adamson, sweaty and breathing hard from basketball practice, was waiting for Nancy when she came out of the locker room. Each time she saw him, her breath caught in her throat. It wasn't just that he was attractive. It was that she still couldn't believe her luck in having him transfer from Garrison, a rival school, to Tarenton High. True, this second time around, they'd gotten off to a rocky start. As center on the Tarenton Wolves basketball team, he'd been pressured by old friends and ex-teammates at Garrison into shaving points for money when the rival teams played each other. If he'd done it, that would have blitzed their relationship right then and there. But he hadn't. And that had told her what she needed to know about him.

Nancy Goldstein didn't ordinarily think of herself as being lucky. Most of what she had, she took for granted: a lovely home, parents who cared about her (and while that was often annoying, she knew it was better than having them *not* care), and a position in school that many other girls envied. But Ben Adamson's transfer to Tarenton High made her feel like her lucky star had been working overtime. Her relationship with Ben, full of excitement and newness and, finally, laughter, made her past romance with Josh Breitman seem like a brother-sister relationship. Their feelings for each other had gradually cooled, like water in a bathtub, and splitting up had seemed the natural thing to do. And then Ben had shown up. . . .

"Mr. and Mrs. America," Mary Ellen muttered to Pres as they watched Nancy link arms with Ben and walk away from the group. "The pretty cheerleader and the handsome jock. They should be on the cover of *Young Life* magazine."

"Meow!" Pres teased, zipping up the jacket of his pale blue sweat suit. "You sound jealous."

Mary Ellen's mouth dropped open. "*Moi?* Jealous of *her?* Never!"

"Mary Ellen's not jealous," Walt said loyally. "Why should she be? Patrick's nicer than Ben."

Mary Ellen's fair skin turned pink. "Patrick" was one Patrick Henley, the only boy in all of Tarenton who gave Mary Ellen second thoughts about leaving town after graduation. She'd been fighting an emotional tug-of-war with her feelings for a long time — her feelings for great-looking, rugged, friendly Patrick. Everyone liked him. But it wasn't likely that anyone felt quite the same way about him as Mary Ellen did.

Unfortunately, Mary Ellen fully intended to kiss Tarenton good-bye one day soon and head for New York City to become a model. Patrick was perfectly happy in Tarenton, though, and kept busy trying to build up his part-time business.

4

Patrick's part-time business was collecting garbage.

Mary Ellen shuddered, just thinking about it. To take her mind off the impossibility of her situation with Patrick, she turned to Angie and asked, "Is Arne picking you up?"

Angie sighed and shook her head. Arne Peterson, tall, thin, and bespectacled, was her boyfriend. "No, he's got computer time this afternoon."

"Honestly, Angie," Mary Ellen said as they all headed for the showers, "I don't know how you stand it! That boy spends so much time with those computers!" She grinned wickedly. "Pretty soon you're going to have to install a switch on him, just to turn him on. And he doesn't even get *paid* for all that time!"

Money was important to Mary Ellen. Her father was a bus driver, her mother a clerk, and of all the cheerleaders, her budget was the tightest. Only Angie, whose widowed mother ran a beauty parlor in their home, even came close to Mary Ellen's financial situation.

"Arne's trying for a scholarship in a really competitive field," Angie defended her absent boyfriend. "He needs all the computer time he can beg, borrow, or steal."

But Mary Ellen, with her remark about needing a switch to turn Arne on, had hit a very sensitive spot. All the way home in Walt's Jeep later, Angie wished it was that simple: installing a switch. Maybe, she thought, she could have it

5

implanted in his neck, like those little knobs Frankenstein's monster had in those old movies.

If only I were a computer, she thought sadly as she jumped down out of the Jeep and waved good-bye to the others. Arne would want to be with me every single second, instead of just when he doesn't have anything better to do. Maybe if I were even just a typewriter, or a copying machine . . . something! Anything with keys or wires or transistors, she thought as she went into her house, anything that would hold the interest of a scientist like Arne.

Making a face of disgust, she hung her jacket on the rack in the hall and headed for the kitchen to console herself with a fudge brownie. With chocolate frosting. And nuts. And maybe just a smidgen of Rocky Road ice cream. After all, she could always do aerobics for hours after supper, since it wasn't very likely that Arne would tear himself away from his precious computer to call her.

He didn't.

And the following evening, she sat in Arne's car, parked in front of the mall, and listened carefully as he explained why he couldn't see her anymore.

"I just can't afford the time right now, Angie," he explained. His eyes behind wire-rimmed glasses were serious. "These computer experiments in artificial intelligence are being done all over the country. Maybe all over the world. Believe me, the competition is fierce."

"I believe you, Arne," she said quietly. "But I've never complained about how busy you are, have I?"

He shook his head. "No. But you don't have to. I *know* it's not fair to you. You like to have fun, Angie; you like to be around people. And I just don't have the time to do things with you."

Just as she was about to say it didn't matter (even though it did), he added, "And when I'm worried about you sitting at home alone, I can't concentrate. And I can't afford that, Angie. I need a clear head to do this stuff I'm working on."

When she said nothing, just sat there staring at him with round, sad eyes, he said intensely, "You know about competition, right? I mean, being a cheerleader, you see it all the time."

Still she said nothing. He sighed and patted her hand, making her feel about eight years old. "I like being with you, Angie, you know that. You're terrific! I never thought anyone as pretty as you would bother with someone like me. If it was any other time. . . ." He shook his head. "It's just not the right time for me. We just have to cool it for a while, okay?"

No, it wasn't okay. As far as Angie was concerned, the idea stank. Not that she and Arne were the Lovers of the Century. They weren't. Their romance so far had been a lot like a quiet day in the middle of summer, very low-key. Arne had always been seventy-five percent brain and twenty-five percent boyfriend. But that had been enough for her. Having twenty-five percent of someone. she'd figured, was better than having one hundred percent of no one. So she'd tried hard not to complain about the long hours he'd spent in the lab or on the computer.

Now he was taking even that twenty-five percent away from her.

Angie bit her lip, fighting tears. What was it about her. anyway? She just couldn't keep a boy interested in her, was that it? There had been Marc for a while, as dashing and handsome as Arne was smart and trustworthy. But Marc had gone off to college and another girl. He'd found someone else in less time than it takes to say, "Angie Poletti has no sex appeal."

Now Arne was dumping her, too, and it wasn't even for another girl.

She thought, with a sinking heart, Even a stupid machine is more interesting than me!

"You're not mad at me, are you?" Arne asked anxiously. peering into her face. "I hope we can still be friends. I value your friendship. Angie."

He seemed so sincere, and so worried, that she felt sorry for him. Arne was a nice person. Besides, it wasn't *his* fault that she was about as exciting as eating lima beans.

"It's okay, Arne," she said in a dull voice. "Could we just go home now?"

But it *wasn't* okay, she thought later as she hid in the den at her house, away from her mother's worried eyes and her brother Andrew's questions like, "What happened to the brain, anyway? Where is he tonight?"

Why did this have to happen to her? First Marc, now Arne. It didn't happen to the other cheerleaders. Nancy had Ben, and before him she'd had Josh. And Josh hadn't *dumped* Nancy; they'd agreed to split up. But then, why would anyone ever dump someone as pretty and sexy as Nancy Goldstein?

Olivia had Walt, and Walt had Olivia. They'd been together for ages. They'd had their share of problems, but Walt hadn't gone looking for someone else. He'd hung in there, because he really *loved* Olivia.

True, Pres had been dumped by Kerry, but that was his own fault. He just wasn't ready to settle down. Kerry wanted a guy all her own, and Pres tried, but it was too much of a strain on him. And she certainly hadn't dumped him because he was boring! Pres might be a lot of things, but boring wasn't one of them.

As for Mary Ellen, everyone in Tarenton knew that the squad captain, who was so beautiful that she modeled part-time at an expensive boutique in the mall, could have had any boy in town just for the asking. One toss of Mary Ellen's lovely head, one hint from those cornflower-blue eyes, and the line would form to the right. And if Mary Ellen had been ready to commit herself to any one guy (which Angie knew perfectly well she wasn't), the person she'd wink at first would be Patrick Henley.

Look how long he'd been stuck on Mary Ellen, Angie thought with envy as she huddled under an afghan on the couch. Patrick's been hung up on Mary Ellen since the first time he saw her. Sure, he's dated other girls. But wherever he is, if Mary Ellen is there, too, the other girls in the room might just as well pack up and go home. He'll probably *never* give up on her.

Why can't *I* have someone like that? she wondered angrily, tears sliding down her cheeks. I'd be nicer to him than Mary Ellen is to Patrick, that's for sure!

It will always be like that for Mary Ellen, she thought with certainty. Guys will always be tripping over their sneaker laces trying to get to her. They'll be telling her she's beautiful when she's one hundred and one years old!

And that certainty was followed by the depressing thought that the only person in her life who kept telling her how beautiful she was, was . . . her *mother*, for Pete's sake!

She was still thinking about how unfair it all was when she fell asleep.

CHAPTER

The next day at school, it was obvious to everyone who knew them that Angie and Arne were no longer Angie-and-Arne. Her large, dark eyes were pink and swollen in her round, pretty face, and Arne was nowhere to be seen. He didn't show up at lunch as he usually did and she never mentioned his name. She sat at the long table between Pres and Olivia, her food untouched in front of her.

When Olivia asked gently, "You okay, Ange?" she nodded, but her eyes filled with tears. Giving Nancy and Mary Ellen a strange look of resentment, she stuffed her still-wrapped sandwich back into its paper bag, mumbled something about needing to go to the library, and left the cafeteria.

After a silent, awkward moment at the table,

Pres asked, "What's with her? She sure is in a rotten mood!" He grinned. "Maybe Body-Snatchers have invaded her and stolen her usually cheerful personality."

"It's not funny, Pres," Olivia said. "Sometimes I think you have the sensitivity of a chain-link fence! Can't you see she's really feeling bad? I think Arne broke up with her."

Pres shrugged his sizable shoulders. "He's not her type, anyway. Angie's a lot of fun, and Arne's idea of a good time is indexing floppy discs."

"Maybe," Olivia said thoughtfully, "but Angie really cared about him."

Mary Ellen, sandwich halfway to her mouth, looked at Nancy and asked, "Did you see that look she gave us before she left?"

Nancy nodded. "Yeah. What was that all about? What did you do to her?"

"I haven't done *anything* to her!" Mary Ellen answered in protest. "Why would I do anything to Angie?"

"Well, *I* haven't done anything. But that look she gave us would have turned the Rock of Gibraltar into a puddle of pudding."

"I think I'll go see if I can find her," Olivia said, getting up. "Maybe I can cheer her up."

"That's a good idea," Walt agreed. "I'll go with you."

When they'd gone, Pres said, "Well, if anyone can cheer her up, it's Walt. That's his specialty."

Mary Ellen and Nancy nodded. Walt *was* a champion at making people smile. They all

12

figured it had something to do with his parents being in "show business," hosting a local television talk show from their lovely log cabin in the woods. They weren't sure if Walt had inherited his ability to entertain, or developed it as a defense mechanism to compete for his folks' attention. Either way, Walt was more fun at a party than a dozen video games. And he was a good friend to have.

"Walt will have Angie grinning in no time," Nancy said, brushing crumbs from her lap.

"I hope so," Mary Ellen said grimly. "If she's like that tomorrow afternoon at the pep rally, we'll have the student body crying in sympathy instead of cheering!"

But the pep rally wasn't until tomorrow. Anything could happen before then, Mary Ellen told herself as she rode the bus to her job at the mall. Arne could realize what he's letting go of, and run back to Angie and fix everything. If there's one thing we *don't* need now, it's trouble on the squad, and if Arne causes it, I will personally see to it that every computer in the school short-circuits on him!

Mrs. Gunderson, Mary Ellen's boss at Marnie's, gave her a raspberry knit top and skirt to wear while she posed on the little platform outside the store. The tall, elegant woman with hair the same color as Mary Ellen's, fastened in a chic chignon, smiled as she handed her model the outfit.

"It's a good color on you," she said. "Knock 'em dead!"

Mary Ellen grinned. Although standing on the platform for hours at a time was often boring and a lot harder than she'd expected, wearing the gorgeous clothes from Marnie's made it more interesting. Since she was saving her money to get to New York, she hadn't been able to buy many of the clothes she modeled, even with the employee's discount Else Gunderson gave her.

She had been on the platform, elegantly posed in the raspberry outfit, for over an hour when she first noticed the young man slouching against the wall opposite Marnie's. Dressed in jeans and an argyle sweater, he was tall and slightly stoop-shouldered, Mary Ellen thought, probably from all the expensive and very professional-looking camera equipment hanging from that part of his body.

The cameras interested her. Cameras always interested Mary Ellen. She was as fond of having her picture taken as she was of running out onto the gym floor in her red wool skirt with the white pleats, and her white sweater with the big red "T" on the front. Sometimes she felt she'd been born to do both. But you couldn't go on leading cheers for the rest of your life, and that's where the cameras came in. Being a model didn't last forever, either, but if you were really good, you could make enough money to do other things when the modeling ended.

The man was probably in his early twenties,

she figured. He had a roundish face under very short blond hair, almost punk in cut. His lower lip jutted out a little. He looks like a little boy, she thought with surprise. How can someone so tall look like a little boy?

When she looked up again, he was gone. Good. She'd never seen him before and, photographer or not, she was not allowed to talk to anyone while she was working, especially strangers. Else Gunderson had told her more than once, "Just because you're on public view on that platform, some people will think you're accessible to them. Celebrities deal with that sort of thing all the time, and it can be annoying. It's up to you to discourage it."

And he *had* been staring at her. She was sure she hadn't imagined that. She was glad he was gone.

But when she jumped down from the platform five minutes before Marnie's' closing time, there he was, at her elbow, saying, "Excuse me, Miss, could I talk to you for a second?"

Mary Ellen glanced around for a glimpse of the brown uniforms of the security guards.

Seeing her hesitation, the young man added quickly, "It's okay. I'm not a nut, honest. Here!" And he thrust out one hand. In it was a small, white business card.

Mary Ellen took it. It read simply: REESE OLIVER, PHOTOGRAPHY. There was no address or telephone number.

She looked up at him with interest. Mrs. Gund-

15

erson, a former model herself, had told her that she would need a portfolio of pictures of herself to take with her to modeling agencies. She had said it would be expensive, but it was absolutely essential.

And thanks to a great-aunt she had hardly known, she did have a little money now. It was gathering dust and interest in a special account at the Tarenton Savings and Loan on Main Street.

It wouldn't hurt to hear what Mr. Reese Oliver had to say. She had a few minutes before Else turned out the store lights and locked up.

"You're one of the Tarenton cheerleaders, aren't you?" he asked.

She nodded. "Yes. How did you know?"

He shrugged. "I'm a basketball fan. I went to the game the other night."

Tarenton had won, and the squad, she remembered, had been especially good.

"You look really great up there on that platform," he said, pointing toward it. "You make a great model. I knew you would when I saw you at the game. I was hoping you'd think about letting me shoot you."

She laughed. "Shoot me? That sounds scary!"

He still hadn't smiled. His eyes were pale, almost colorless, with pale lashes and thick, reddish eyebrows.

"That's photographer talk," he explained very seriously. "I mean, I'd like you to pose for me. I thought, since you're already modeling here, you might even be interested in having a complete portfolio done. I do that kind of thing all the time."

"Here? In Tarenton?" That seemed unlikely to Mary Ellen. How many would-be models could there be in a small town?

He shrugged again. "All over the place. I travel a lot. That's one of the best things about being a photographer," he added proudly. "The traveling."

"Well, who do you work *for*?" she asked, glancing toward Marnie's briefly to see if Else was still there.

She was behind the cash register, her head bent.

"I work for *me*. On assignment, mostly. Magazines contact me and give me jobs to do. I do a lot of free-lance work."

Hmm . . . that would make it harder to check him out, the way she knew her parents — *and* Else — would expect her to.

"Do you live here? In Tarenton?" She really should find out *something* about him.

His colorless eyes looked away, focusing on the fountain behind Mary Ellen. "Like I said," he reminded her, "I move around a lot. I have a room at the Tarenton Motel right now, just outside of town."

A warning bell rang in Mary Ellen's head. "Do you have a studio here in town?" she asked pointedly. Did she really look so stupid that he would think for one minute that he could get her to a motel room just like that?

17

His pale cheeks flushed. "Look, what's with the third degree? There's no point in my renting a studio here. I won't *be* here that long. I've got a cover shoot for *American Sports* magazine already assigned and I'll be moving on pretty soon to do that."

She raised her eyebrows. It would be easy enough to check *that* out. "Do you have a crew with you?"

He blinked. "A crew? No, there's just me. I'm not a television reporter," he said in a tone of voice that implied she probably had an I.Q. no higher than ten. "They're the only ones who use camera crews."

She felt incredibly stupid. Still, she hesitated. She was really going to need that portfolio. Running into a professional photographer was a stroke of luck, like the money her great-aunt had left her. But a motel room, alone, with a stranger. . . . Well, wasn't that just the kind of situation parents warned their daughters about all the time? *Her* parents never had, of course, because never in their wildest dreams would they expect her to run into such a situation.

"Look, I — " she began, but he interrupted her. Putting his hands up, palms toward her, he said, "Listen, why don't we just forget it, okay? I can see you're not wild about the idea."

"No, it's not that, I — "

"I don't need to browbeat people into posing for me, okay? If I hadn't seen you at the game and again on the platform there, I would have

18

just gone on about my business. And I think that's what I'll do now. Sorry I bothered you."

He turned to go, the heavy camera equipment pulling one shoulder lower than the other.

"No, wait!" Mary Ellen called. Mrs. Gunderson turned off the overhead neon sign and peered through the glass door. "Listen, just let me go home and check out my schedule, okay? I'll call you at the motel, I promise, just as soon as I can figure out how to fit it in."

He paused and looked back at her. "Well, if you're sure. . . ."

"I'm sure."

"It might help if I knew your name."

Oh, heavens! He must be wondering how someone as stupid as she was, was allowed out of the house. "Mary Ellen Kirkwood."

"Fine. Mary Ellen Kirkwood. If you call, fine. I just don't like having people think I'm trying to browbeat them into something, that's all."

"I don't," she protested, thinking of the portfolio. "I'm sorry if I acted that way. I promise I'll call you as soon as I know when I can do it."

"Sure. If I'm not there, just leave a message with the guy at the desk."

"Right. See you. And thanks!"

He turned away as she hurried into the store to change her clothes. Then he left the mall.

He had almost reached his car in the parking lot when he saw, just ahead of him, another cheerleader. This one had brown hair but was almost as pretty as Mary Ellen Kirkwood.

19

He hadn't expected to run into two cheerleaders in one night.

The parking lot was well lit and there were plenty of people around, going to their cars, so he took a chance and approached her, business card in hand, as she opened the door of a dark blue sedan.

"I didn't mean to scare you," he apologized as she jumped when he called out to her. He *had* frightened her, even with all of the other people around.

"I was just talking to one of your co-cheerleaders," he said, as she stood in tan tailored slacks, turtleneck sweater, and a heavy white jacket, with her back against the car door, staring at him. "Mary Ellen? Kirkwood?"

She nodded, noticing the cameras, and visibly relaxing. He was probably from the newspaper.

"And you're. . . ?"

"Nancy Goldstein. What do you want? Are you a friend of Mary Ellen's?"

He shook his head. "Not really. I just met her." Handing her his business card, he explained awkwardly that he would like to photograph her. But he was annoyed by the way she handled his business card, gingerly, by the edges, as if it were a leaflet handed her by a religious cult.

Nancy Goldstein hadn't been raised to talk to strangers any more than Mary Ellen had, and she didn't share Mary Ellen's desire to be a model. Ben was waiting for her, and she didn't feel like wasting time with some person she'd never seen in her life before, whether Mary Ellen knew him or not. She couldn't think of a single reason why she should talk to this man.

"Sorry," she said, turning away to open the car door. "I'm not interested in having my picture taken." That was the kind of thing her mother had taught her to say to door-to-door salesmen, in just that sort of firm, no-nonsense voice.

"But — "

"No. I'm really not. Thanks, anyway."

And she got into the car and drove away, leaving him standing in the middle of the parking lot.

A traveling photographer? She'd never heard of anything like that before. Had Mary Ellen agreed to pose for him? Probably. Mary Ellen turning down a chance to be photographed was as unlikely as Walt turning down a party, Pres turning down a pretty girl, Angie refusing chocolate. . . .

And just who *was* this Reese Oliver person, anyway?

She hoped Mary Ellen had had the good sense to check him out thoroughly before she'd agreed to anything. He looked respectable enough, but he *was* a stranger, after all.

CHAPTER

When Mary Ellen got home that night, she headed straight for the magazine rack in the living room. She knew her father occasionally got a copy of *American Sports* magazine, and prayed he'd done so recently.

He had. It was the third magazine from the front and it didn't take her long to find what she was looking for inside. It was right there on the "Table of Contents" page, under "Photographic Credits," his name in black and white: Reese Oliver.

She sat back on the couch, the magazine open on her lap. So, he'd been telling the truth. Well, she'd known that all along, hadn't she? But it had just seemed too good to be true — first the money from her great-aunt, and now a real, honest-togoodness professional photographer showing up in Tarenton.

Everything is going exactly the way I want it to, she thought happily, leafing through the telephone book for the number of the motel. With a really good portfolio and what's left of my inheritance after I pay for the pictures, I'll be on my way out of Tarenton sooner than I'd thought.

There had been so many times lately when she had almost given up hope of ever making it to New York.

"I'm sorry," a nasal voice interrupted her thoughts. "Room three-fourteen does not answer. May I take a message?"

Mary Ellen left her name and number, regretting now that she hadn't accepted Reese Oliver's offer right away. Suppose he'd already found someone else to photograph?

Telling herself that was just plain silly, that the streets of Tarenton weren't exactly crawling with photogenic females, she waited by the telephone.

But he didn't call her back that night. She finally gave up and went to bed, mentally scolding herself for being such a dope.

"Dope! Dope! Dope!" she muttered under her breath, as she brushed her hair until it felt like silk.

When she fell asleep, she dreamed, as she did so often, that she was the toast of New York City, gracing the covers of fashion magazines, showing up on talk shows, and being taken to all the best restaurants.

Only this time, Reese Oliver appeared in the very best part of her dream, shaking his head no and calling out in a thunderous voice, "No! No! Not her! Get her out of here and keep her out! I've found somebody better!"

She didn't sleep very well.

At the pep rally the next afternoon, it quickly became obvious to everyone that Angie's mind was not on her cartwheels or her flips or pikes. Or on anything going on in the gym, for that matter.

"Gee, Angie," Walt finally complained mildly, when the naturally athletic Angie had mistimed her dismount from his back and landed badly. "What's with you?"

Fortunately the pep rally was over because, to his horror, the cheerleader he liked more than anyone except Olivia, burst into tears and ran off the floor and out of the gym.

"What'd I say?" Walt cried. "What'd I do?"

Pres shrugged as they all headed for the locker rooms. "Who knows? Girls!" He was between girls himself at the moment, an unusual state of affairs for the rich and handsome Preston Tilford III. Far too often to suit him now, he drove around town with nothing in the Porsche but him and the smooth gray upholstery. The situation was making him edgy. Pres without a girl was like a car needing its battery charged — he did what he was supposed to do, but not well.

Mary Ellen looked at Nancy as Angie ran out of the gym, and repeated Pres's shrug. "Has to be Arne," she said, and Nancy nodded.

In the locker room, Angie explained tearfully why she was upset.

"Gee, I'm sorry, Angie," Mary Ellen said as Olivia, who already knew about the breakup, sat with her arm around Angie's shoulders. "Maybe he'll change his mind."

"Why would she want him to?" Nancy asked sharply. "Anyone who prefers a computer to Angie isn't nearly as smart as everyone says he is!"

Mary Ellen nodded as she checked her hair in the mirror. She bent forward from the waist to brush it from the roots down to fluff it, talking to the others as she worked.

"You can find somebody better than Arne, Angie," she said through a cloud of cornsilk. "Somebody whose idea of fun isn't just pushing little keys."

Angie glanced up and gave both Mary Ellen and Nancy the same look of resentment they'd seen in the cafeteria the day before.

"What would either of *you* know about it?" she blurted out, surprising all of them. "Nancy, you've got Ben, and Olivia's got Walt. And Mary Ellen, you could have Patrick any time you crooked your little finger at him."

They stared at her, as she stood up and her voice rose. "Even if you don't want Patrick," she continued, facing an astonished Mary Ellen, "the line of boys waiting for a chance with you would circle the high school. And," she added, her round cheeks very pink, "it's a very *big* school! So just don't tell me I shouldn't care about Arne. Because he *was* the line of boys waiting for me!"

"We were just trying to help," Mary Ellen said in an offended voice, as she fastened a bright red ribbon around the front of her head to keep the cloud of pale hair away from her face.

"Hey, guys!" Olivia said quickly, standing up. "Let's cool it! We've got a game in just a little while. Maybe we'd better concentrate on that, okay? Angie?"

Breathing hard, Angie sat back down. "Sorry," she said softly, "I'm sorry. I shouldn't be yelling at anyone."

"That's okay," Mary Ellen mumbled, stuffing her brush into her knapsack.

"Why don't we all go get something to eat?" Olivia suggested. "As my mother would say, our bodies need fuel."

"Okay," Mary Ellen agreed, "but I've got to make a phone call first. Wait for me outside."

She had slipped the motel telephone number and Reese's business card into the side of her red and white saddle shoes and had already called him twice that day. There had been no answer.

This time, she let it ring at least a dozen times, with no luck. The motel switchboard operator didn't pick up on the call, so she couldn't leave a message. Well, he wouldn't be able to reach her during the game, anyway. She'd have to call him when she got home.

Hurrying outside to meet the others, she wondered where Reese Oliver was spending all of his free time. Had he already made friends in Tarenton? He hadn't seemed that outgoing to her. He was probably just out taking pictures.

Of *who?*

Several hours later, after they'd all made their peace at a nearby salad bar and psyched themselves up for the game with Deep River, she discovered where Reese Oliver was.

He was in the bleachers of the Tarenton High School gym. She spotted him right in the middle of a cheer, as Ben Adamson raced down the court with the ball toward the Deep River basket, dribbling furiously.

"Raise that score!" Mary Ellen shouted with the rest. Catching sight of Oliver in the stands, her eyes widened as her skirt whirled around her, the white pleats flaring out against the red wool.

"More! More! More!"

What was he *doing* here? Looking for her? she hoped.

"Take the floor! More! More! More!"

Could she catch him after the game?

"Take the floor and raise that score!"

* * *

27

The ball went in, bobbled around, and sank through the net, making the score Tarenton, 8; Deep River, 4.

Mary Ellen ran back to the first bleacher where they sat between cheers, keeping her eyes on Reese Oliver. She could hardly wait to talk to him and get it all settled. Going to his motel room for the photo sessions wasn't a problem. She would simply take someone with her. Maybe her younger sister, Gemma. And with Gemma there, Mary Ellen would be perfectly safe.

Although Reese Oliver had looked perfectly harmless to her.

Maybe she could catch him at halftime.

In the stands, Reese Oliver turned to the boy standing next to him and asked politely, "Excuse me. Do you happen to know the names of the cheerleaders? The Tarenton ones?"

The boy stared at him. "Well, sure," he said. "Doesn't everybody?"

Reese shook his head. "I'm new here. Who's the cute one?"

The boy laughed. "Are you kidding? Who *isn't* cute?"

"No, I mean the one with long, blonde hair."

"Oh, yeah. That's Mary Ellen Kirkwood. I wouldn't call her 'cute,' though. Mary Ellen's a real knockout."

"No," Reese said impatiently, "not her. The *other* one. The healthy-looking one."

"Oh, that's Angie Poletti. She's a good kid.

28

Seems kind of off on her timing tonight, though. She's usually perfect."

As far as Reese was concerned, she *was* perfect. Even from a distance she had a trusting, open look the other girls lacked. The camera would love her, he knew it. He could tell. She was exactly what he'd been looking for.

He could get her address out of the telephone book. And this time, he'd go to her house instead of approaching her in public, like someone trying to sell her something. No wonder the other two had been suspicious about him. He should have been more businesslike.

At halftime, Ardith Engborg pulled Angie aside and, speaking in a low voice, said, "Anythink wrong, Angie?" Ardith knew her cheerleaders very well, well enough to sense a lack of concentration on Angie's part. The girl was an incredibly well-tuned athlete, yet she'd nearly fallen during that last flying angel. And it was obvious, at least to Ardith, that she hadn't been doing her part during her side stands on Walt's thigh. The strain had shown in his face.

"It's nothing, Mrs. Engborg," Angie said quietly. "I guess I've been kind of out of it. I'm sorry. I'll snap out of it. I promise."

Only a little reassured, Ardith sighed and left to get something to drink. Being in a hot and crowded gym always made her thirsty. And dealing constantly with the emotional problems of six healthy, active young people made her crazy. I can't do anything about the crazy part, she thought as she approached the water fountain in the hall, but I can at least do something about the thirsty part.

While Ardith was getting a drink and Angie was doing some limbering-up exercises with renewed vigor, Mary Ellen searched the crowd for Reese Oliver.

But instead of looking into a pair of colorless eyes, she found herself face-to-face with a stubborn, rugged chin and deep blue, laughing eyes.

"Patrick! Hi! I didn't know you were here."

"Mary Ellen." He grinned at her and threw an arm around her shoulders. "When have I ever missed a game? It's the perfect opportunity to stare at you all I want without anyone thinking I'm weird."

Mary Ellen was glad to see Patrick. She was always glad to see him. Why wouldn't she be? Patrick Henley, with his good looks and charm, decorated Tarenton High School like lights on a Christmas tree. He'd only been absent two or three days that she could remember, and those days had seemed just plain *gray*.

But right now she needed to see Reese Oliver.

"Lose something?" Patrick asked, noticing that her eyes were scanning the crowded gym.

"Oh. No, sorry." Reese Oliver would have to wait. She'd never find him in this crowd, anyway. She'd just have to call him later.

Looking up at Patrick with her super-voltage smile ("guaranteed to short-circuit the electricity for twenty miles around," Patrick had told her once), she said, "Buy me a Coke?"

He nodded and gave her a hug.

To find Reese Oliver, Mary Ellen would have had to look in a phone booth in the front hall. He was leafing through the Tarenton phone book, murmuring, "Poletti, Poletti. . . ."

CHAPTER

Mary Ellen was in high spirits during the second half of the game. Angie had regained her timing, Tarenton was slaughtering Deep River, Patrick would be waiting after the game to take her home, and there was still Reese Oliver and his promise of a portfolio. She felt terrific.

The six cheerleaders, megaphones in hand, ran out onto the sidelines as Deep River grabbed a rebound. Mary Ellen, elastic with nervous energy, led the cheer, her pale hair flying out behind her.

"Steal it, steal it,
Take it away!"

And when Deep River made the basket and Ben Adamson caught the ball, heading back down the floor, the Varsity cheerleaders shouted,

"Up and in!
Watch us win!
Up and in!"

Patrick, watching Mary Ellen from the stands, grinned down at her, thinking she had never looked prettier.

Reese Oliver, sitting just a few rows from Patrick, was thinking how glad he was that the other two cheerleaders hadn't leaped at his offer to photograph them, because his camera was going to love Angie Poletti. She was perfect. Just perfect!

Tarenton beat Deep River, 48 to 42.

Even Angie's spirits had lifted. During the last half she hadn't thought about Arne even once.

But when Nancy and Ben, and Olivia and Walt invited her to go for pizza with them, she began to feel like the fifth wheel on a pair of roller skates. So she said no thanks, and let Mary Ellen and Patrick drop her off at home.

In the darkness, none of them noticed the blue compact car parked at the corner as they pulled into Angie's driveway to let her out.

When Angie had gone into the house and flipped off the porch light, Patrick drove Mary Ellen home. But she didn't get out of the truck right away. She never got out of the truck right away. Being with Patrick, sitting close to him high up on the front seat of his garbage truck, gave her a feeling of warmth and comfort she never had at any other time.

And being in Patrick's arms, as she knew she was about to be, made her see flashing colored lights in her head. Each time she found herself with Patrick, it became harder to remember what he did for a living. For a long time, just picturing Patrick in his white coveralls, tossing the contents of someone's metal trash can into the back of his truck, had been enough to make her pull away.

More and more often now, that didn't work. Patrick seemed sexier to her every time she saw him, and when he held her, it felt *good*. That was all — it just felt really good.

And tonight was no exception. By the time the colored lights began flashing, Mary Ellen's knees were weak and her breathing would have caused concern at the local emergency center.

Then she remembered how close she was to getting what she wanted: the portfolio, followed by escape from Tarenton. Getting really involved with Patrick now would be as stupid as dropping out of a race just a few steps from the finish line. She wasn't that stupid, was she?

"No, Patrick," she murmured, pushing gently against his chest.

With a loud groan and what looked like a lot of effort on his part, he let her go and leaned back against the seat. He shook his head, hard. "Okay, okay," he said shakily, his own breathing none too even. "I was waiting for that. And you're right. A garbage truck is just not the place for romance."

She liked Patrick too much to tell him that it wasn't the place, it was the *situation*. The ending would have been the same no matter where they'd been. It was the situation she couldn't handle. Shouldn't handle. Didn't *want* to handle.

"Patrick," she said in a husky voice, "I think I need to go into my house. That house, the house right there in front of us. I need to go in there. And you need to stay out here."

"Gotcha!" he said, grinning. "But one of these nights, Mary Ellen. . . ."

"Maybe. But not tonight. It's late and I'm tired."

And I need to make a very important telephone call, she added silently.

After one last, very thorough kiss, she got down from the truck and went inside.

But again, there was no answer at the motel. Doesn't the guy ever sleep? she wondered angrily, slamming down the phone. At this rate, by the time he took his pictures, she'd have gray hair and her face would look like a baggy sweater! Where *was* he, anyway?

Where he was, was at Angie Poletti's house. Mary Ellen would have been surprised to learn not only that he was there, but that he was smiling. He hadn't smiled at her even once.

He was smiling because Angie's mouth was open almost as wide as her dark eyes. The Poletti living room was well lit, and he was delighted to find that he'd been right about her. She was even prettier up close than she had been from a distance.

"You want to take pictures of *me*?" she cried.

He nodded. He had already explained that he was a professional photographer and that he had seen her at the game earlier that night. "You're exactly what I'm looking for," he said. "You'd make a wonderful model. That is, if you're interested."

Angie sank into a chair. Then, remembering her manners, she motioned for him to do the same.

"But I'm . . . I'm not the model type," she protested. "Didn't you *see* the other cheerleaders? Mary Ellen and Nancy would be better models than I would. Even Olivia, except she's too tiny."

After all, she was thinking, my own boyfriend doesn't even want me anymore. Why would anybody else?

"I was there tonight," he said calmly, "and I saw all of you. I've already talked to two of your co-cheerleaders," he added honestly, "and you're the one I want."

She knew which two. Frowning, she wondered what had happened. Mary Ellen wouldn't turn down a chance to be photographed, would she? Not in a zillion years!

At the same time, she couldn't believe that any photographer who had good eyesight would pass up the chance to photograph either Nancy *or* Mary Ellen — certainly not to take pictures of *her*.

36

"I'm not looking for sophistication," he explained.

Well, that certainly explains why you're talking to *me*! Angie thought dryly.

"I don't even have any cheekbones," she said with a short laugh.

"You have what's marketable right now," he said firmly. "Good health. Physical fitness. A magazine won't sell today if it doesn't contain at least one article on physical fitness. Diet, exercise — you name it. Any magazine with *your* picture on the cover would sell like crazy."

Angie was having trouble digesting what this long, tall, rabbity-looking young man was telling her. She was no model. She wasn't even that pretty. Or was she? Shouldn't he know what he was talking about? A professional photographer wouldn't go around taking pictures of ugly people, would he?

She wished her mother hadn't left the room. After Reese had surprised both of them by ringing the doorbell, introducing himself, and asking to speak to Angie, her mother had chatted for a few minutes and then left for the kitchen. She probably figured I already knew him, Angie thought. Maybe she even thought he was a new boyfriend.

No way. He wasn't her type. He was at least five years older than she was, for one thing. And although he was still talking about physical fitness, *he* wasn't physically fit. He was very pale, and his body didn't seem to have a lot of bone or muscle. He reminded her of an unbaked breadstick. He wasn't ugly; in fact he was kind of cute in a rabbity sort of way. But definitely not her type.

". . . cover for *American Sports* magazine coming up. If I had a portfolio of you, I could blow up a few of the best shots and suggest they use you."

A magazine cover? Her? No, that was Mary Ellen's goal, not hers. He had the wrong house, the wrong room, the wrong cheerleader.

She told him so.

"No," he said firmly, surprising her by suddenly developing a strong, stubborn jaw. "I have the *right* cheerleader. You're perfect for today. Of course, if you're not interested. . . ."

She hesitated. It might be nice to have something new and fun in her life right now, besides cheerleading. And she *was* flattered. Hadn't he just said she was "perfect"? How many guys in her life had told her that? She could count them on no hands.

"What would I have to do?"

He leaned forward in his chair. "Well, the first thing is the portfolio. That's a collection of still shots. You need that before you can take step one in modeling. Listen, I'll only charge you half the going rate, okay? Because I think you've really got something."

Oh. She hadn't realized she'd need money.

38

Well, she did have some saved. But just exactly what was the going rate?

"We'll do a good-sized package to begin with," he added, "enough for you to see what I mean about you being perfect for today's market. It won't cost you that much, and it'll give me enough to take to the magazine. How about it?"

Why not? If the time ever came when her picture was on the cover of a national magazine, on newstands all across the country, Marc and Arne would see it. Wouldn't she just love to see the look on their faces when she stared out at them from some magazine display?

And wouldn't Mary Ellen just *die* when she found out?

Scolding herself for being so catty, she asked Reese Oliver for a dollar amount and he gave it to her. It was a figure she could afford.

"Okay," she said, grinning. "I'll do it. When do we start?"

He stood up, and she did, too. "Well, here's the thing," he said very seriously. "I make it a policy to get to know my subjects really well before I snap the shutter."

Subjects? Shutter? He sounded so professional. He must really know what he was doing. She was glad she'd said yes.

"Maybe you could show me around town," he suggested, "since I really don't know the place. That way, I'd become more familiar with both my surroundings and my subject. Okay?"

She nodded, wondering at the same time how she would fit a tour of Tarenton into an already-busy schedule. Well, she'd manage. Good thing Tarenton was a small town!

"Should I get my hair cut or anything?" she asked anxiously as she led him to the front door. "Or my mom could give me a perm. She has a beauty parlor right downstairs."

Whirling around to face her, he said in a loud voice, "No! No! Don't do *anything*! For Pete's sake, you'd ruin everything. Don't change one single hair. Didn't you hear me say you're perfect just the way you are?"

Yes, she'd heard him. She just found it hard to believe, that was all.

When he had gone, Angie danced around the living room, her blonde hair flying out around her face as she twirled. A person of the male persuasion had said she was "perfect." Perfect! She wasn't ugly after all — even if Arne *didn't* want her.

And this person, who was a professional photographer from out-of-town (meaning from someplace far more exciting than Tarenton), wanted to put her on the cover of a national magazine. Her! Angie Poletti!

At least, she thought happily as she walked down the hall toward her room, he wanted to try. When she had changed into her robe and pajamas, she would go tell her mother all about it. *She* probably wouldn't find it so hard to believe. She was always telling Angie how pretty she was.

40

But then, she thought, what can you expect from a mother?

Reese wasn't her mother, though. He wasn't even related to her. And *he* thought she would make a good model!

CHAPTER

Angie Poletti had a heart as sweet as a marshmallow. And in spite of her feelings about Mary Ellen "just dying" from envy, if she had seen the look on her squad captain's face later that evening during the phone conversation with the photographer, she would have gone to him and begged him to photograph Mary Ellen instead of herself.

Mary Ellen's voice was full of relief when, finally, Reese Oliver's voice said, "Hello." It was the fifth time she'd called the motel that night. Her frustration at having given up time in Patrick's arms to repeatedly dial an unanswered number was giving her a headache.

"Oh, I'm so glad you're there!" she cried. "I've been calling you all night. And yesterday. And . . . well, never mind. That's not important."

"Who is this?" he asked politely.

"Mary Ellen Kirkwood," she said quickly. "You wanted to photograph me, remember? At the mall? I was modeling for Marnie's?"

"Oh, yeah. You turned me down."

Oh, dear. "No, no, I didn't." Mary Ellen gripped the receiver tightly. It was important to say exactly the right thing. She couldn't admit she'd been suspicious. "I just had to check to see when I'd have time. And I *have* been trying to reach you. Didn't you get my messages?"

"Ah . . . no, I guess not."

Her hand felt clammy on the receiver. He didn't sound all that happy to hear her voice. Why hadn't she jumped at the chance to model for him when he first offered it?

"Well, I *do* have time," she said, her lips stiff with anxiety. "I just have to juggle a few things around. You probably have to do that sometimes yourself, right?" she added, her voice full of hope.

There was a moment of silence. She held her breath, waiting for him to say, Oh, sure. I understand. Listen, that's just great. When can we set up the first session?

He *had* to say that! He just had to.

He didn't say anything like that. What he said instead was, "Gee, I'm sorry, Mary Ellen. I'm afraid I've found someone else."

So there they were, ringing in her ears: six simple little words that drained every ounce of color from Mary Ellen's face, leaving her lovely complexion the color of smoke.

43

No. It wasn't possible. Not in such a short time. Who could he have found?

"But I. . . ." her voice sounded weak and breathless to her own ears.

"I'm sorry. I thought you weren't interested. I mean, you weren't exactly wild with enthusiasm, you know."

Mary Ellen felt as if she was sinking into a deep, dark hole while clutching at a greased rope. That portfolio was her rope to success and she couldn't believe she was losing her grip on it.

A portfolio could have made all the difference in the world to her. It could have sped things up, made things easier.

If a speeding train had roared through the Kirkwoods' living room at that precise moment, Mary Ellen would have thrown herself under it.

"But I don't understand," she said weakly. "The other night you sounded so sure."

"That was the other night." His voice came over the line as matter-of-factly as if she had just asked him for the time. Every word hit her over the head like a club. "I did say I would only be here a little while, Mary Ellen. I couldn't afford to wait for your answer. Time is money, right? It takes time to set up a shoot."

"But I'll *make* the time," she argued, wondering at the same time if it sounded like she was begging. Well, she *was* begging. Some things were worth begging for, and this was definitely one of them. She knew that the minute the con-

versation ended, so did her chances at that portfolio.

"I'm sorry." His voice was very final. "If you'd
called sooner. . . ."

"I tried," she reminded him quietly. She knew
it was no use. He was no longer interested in
photographing Miss Mary Ellen Kirkwood.

"I'm sorry," he said again.

It wasn't until she'd hung up and left the
kitchen that she realized she hadn't asked him
who his new model was.

Lying on her bed, disappointment weighing
her down like a cement blanket, she thought
about who the rat fink might be who had taken
her place in front of Reese Oliver's camera. What
low-life in Tarenton had stolen from her the
opportunity of a lifetime?

Vanessa Barlow.

Mary Ellen sat up straight in bed.

It had to be Vanessa. Tall, exotic-looking
Vanessa, thin-as-a-rail Vanessa — Vanessa with
the long, silky black veil of hair cascading down
her back. The job at Marnie's had originally been
hers because Mary Ellen hadn't been able to fit it
into her schedule. But Vanessa had blown it by
goofing off, and Marnie's owner had then changed
the schedule to fit Mary Ellen's needs.

She lay back down and groaned, burying her
head in the pillow just as her younger sister
Gemma came into the room.

"Gosh, Mary Ellen, what's wrong? Are you

45

sick?" Gemma cried, striding on long, thin legs to stand beside Mary Ellen's bed.

"Yes!" her sister shouted from the folds of the pillow. "Yes, yes, yes!" Pulling the pillow away from her face, "I am sick of — of — things!"

Gemma stared at her. Then she giggled. "Well, that sure pins it down."

Mary Ellen gave her a dark look and Gemma retreated to her own bed. Sitting down, she said remorsefully, "I'm sorry, Mary Ellen, I shouldn't have laughed. You just looked so *mad*!"

"Be quiet now, Gemma," Mary Ellen ordered calmly. "I need to concentrate on the best way to murder someone."

They were quiet for a few minutes, Mary Ellen staring up at the ceiling, Gemma's eyes aimlessly wandering over the mess that resulted from two girls sharing a very small bedroom.

Then, giving Mary Ellen an impish look, Gemma said casually, "You could always push the person over a cliff."

Mary Ellen gave her a scornful look. "Be serious! Where am I going to find a cliff in Tarenton?"

Gemma grinned. "K-Mart?"

In spite of herself, Mary Ellen laughed.

Relieved, Gemma pursued the subject. "Sears? U-Rent-It on Main Street? Their ad in the yellow pages says they have everything."

"Stop!" her sister, fighting more laughter, shouted. "Enough! This is a very serious matter. There will be no more joking around, all right?"

Gemma nodded soberly.

Mary Ellen rolled over onto her stomach, making sobbing noises.

"Mary Ellen," Gemma said in a small voice, "I'm sorry. I didn't mean to make you cry." She adored her beautiful older sister and hated seeing her unhappy.

To her astonished delight, Mary Ellen flipped over onto her back again, her face fighting a grin as she said, "Can't you just see it, Gemma? Me walking into a store and saying, 'Excuse me, Madam, but could you please direct me to your cliffs department? I am especially interested in the kind used for pushing people off . . . of . . . from' . . . whatever."

And they both dissolved into fits of giggling, laughter that would exhaust Mary Ellen and send her off to sleep without another thought for Reese Oliver *or* his new model.

Reese called Angie early the next morning. Dressed in jeans and an old pink sweat shirt suitable for her Saturday morning household chores, she was just gulping down the last of her toast when the phone rang.

"It's me, Reese," he said when she answered. "How's my favorite model doing this morning?"

It still hadn't sunk in. Catching a glimpse of herself in the mirror over the dining room table, Angie thought, Yeah, right! I could always be the family pet in dog food commercials!

Aloud, she said, "I'm fine. I hope you weren't

planning on taking any pictures of me today, though. Saturday's housekeeping day at the Polettis', and by noon I'm going to look like I've been playing in Patrick's truck!"

"Who's Patrick?"

"Oh, sorry. Just a friend. But the truck he drives is a garbage truck, just to give you the idea."

"Oh. Sure. No, like I told you, we need to get to know each other first. So how about giving me the grand tour tonight? Around seven o'clock? I'll pick you up."

He didn't seem to be leaving much room for discussion about it. Well, why wouldn't she want to go? Now that she'd agreed to pose, and her mother had okayed it, she was anxious to get going on it.

"Sure. That sounds good. I'll be ready."

"Great!" Then he added seriously, "Listen, Angie, how about if we keep this to ourselves, okay?"

"This? What *this*?"

"Well, all of it, for right now. I mean, if you tell your co-cheerleaders that you're going for a modeling career, they might be jealous and that could cause problems for you."

Angie thought about that for a second. Nancy wouldn't be jealous. She didn't have the slightest desire to be a model. And Olivia wasn't interested in much of anything that didn't include either cheerleading or Walt. But Mary Ellen. . . .

"I don't like keeping secrets from my friends," she said slowly.

Wouldn't Mary Ellen hate her when she found out? And what would that do to their friendship? And to the squad? And *why* wasn't Mary Ellen doing this modeling instead of her? She would have to find out. If Mary Ellen had turned Reese down, fine, no problem. She couldn't blame Angie, then, for accepting his offer. But if *he* had turned *her* down. . . . Angie shuddered. Mary Ellen was a nice person, but when she really wanted something, she wanted it fiercely, and it wouldn't be a really terrific idea to get in her way.

"You don't have to keep it a secret forever," Reese said. "Just at first, until we know each other better." He gave a short laugh. "That way, I'll have a chance if they try to talk you out of posing for me."

Angie frowned. "Why would they do that?"

Another short laugh. "Are you kidding? You don't know much about jealousy, do you?"

Now it was her turn to laugh harshly. "Oh, sure I do," she said grimly, feeling again the pain of Marc's abandonment of her for another girl, and Arne's preference for a computer. "Only I've never been on the receiving end before!"

"Well, this time you will be," he said firmly, "and it could get sticky for you. So let's just hold off on spreading the news around for a little while, okay? I don't want my model all upset."

49

"My model." That sounded nice. Plain old Angie Poletti was somebody's model. It felt good. Being somebody's *anything* felt good.

Promising to be ready at seven, she hung up and got busy with her dustrag and vacuum. For the first time in a long while, she was humming.

Mary Ellen, standing on the platform outside Marnie's wearing a teal-blue jersey dress with long sleeves and a turtleneck collar and teal suede boots, spent the entire morning trying to figure out who Reese Oliver could be trying to photograph.

It had to be Vanessa. She dreaded running into her at school on Monday and seeing that smug, triumphant smile when Vanessa announced her news.

I can't deal with that, she thought bitterly. I'll have to quit school. Run away from home. Join the Army. Anything to get me as far away as possible from Vicious Van's Vengeance.

All this time, Vanessa had been waiting for a chance to upset the cheerleaders, because they'd made the Varsity Squad and she hadn't. Being the daughter of the superintendent of schools hadn't given her the berth on the squad that she'd expected.

She'd hated them all ever since.

But why does it have to be *me* she gets her revenge on? Mary Ellen wondered dismally. Not that Vanessa hadn't made the others suffer, too. The rumors she'd spread about the other cheerleaders from time to time had hurt all of them.

By the time Vanessa herself appeared in the main walk of the mall, on her way to Marnie's, Mary Ellen had built up an anger against her that simmered inside her like an active volcano.

So Vanessa's casual, "Hi, Mary Ellen. Bet you're bored to death up there," was met with an angry stare, narrowed eyes, and a grim mouth.

"Heavens!" Vanessa said in surprise, staring up at Mary Ellen as shoppers milled around her. "What's bugging *you*? That evil look you just delivered could have crumbled the Great Wall of China!"

Mary Ellen kept her mouth shut. She would rather have her fingernails torn off, one by one, than give Vanessa the satisfaction of asking what was new in her life. And besides, she knew she couldn't bear to hear the answer.

Vanessa saved her the trouble of asking. "I don't know why you're giving me dirty looks," she said, "but if it's any consolation, I'm every bit as bored with life as I know you are up there."

Bored? With the prospect of a magazine cover staring her in the face? How could that be?

"So," Vanessa added lazily, "I'm going to thrill your boss by buying a whole new outfit. Anything to break up the monotony of a dull Saturday. See you later."

And she was gone, her black leather trousers making a whispering sound as she walked away.

Mary Ellen's frown deepened. If Vanessa was really Reese Oliver's new model, the first person

51

she would have told was Mary Ellen. She would have shouted it for all the mall to hear.

She had definitely not sounded like a person who had something new and exciting in her life, especially something that she knew someone else wanted. She wouldn't have kept her mouth shut about that.

Mary Ellen stared after Vanessa. If Vanessa wasn't Reese Oliver's new model, then who *was*?

CHAPTER

Ruling out Vanessa left Mary Ellen with mixed feelings. While she was so relieved that it wasn't Vanessa, it left her knees weak, because that would have been worse than having her hair turn purple overnight or failing every single one of her classes or learning that Patrick had eloped. But she was still being driven crazy by not knowing who it *was*.

After changing from the teal-blue dress into black satin trousers and a cream-colored satin blouse with long, billowy sleeves, she resumed her place on the platform.

When Patrick showed up she was still frowning, concentrating her mental energy on every pretty face she knew, trying to decide which of them might have taken away from her what she'd wanted.

"What's the problem?" he asked, smiling up at her. "Your gorgeous face has trouble written all over it." He looked terrific in neatly pressed chinos and a pale blue V-neck sweater over an open-collared tan shirt. He must have finished collecting for the day.

If anyone could take her mind off her troubles, it was Patrick Henley. He'd done it a million times before.

With a huge effort, she pushed the pretty faces of Tarenton out of her head and gave Patrick a weak smile. So Reese Oliver didn't want her. Patrick certainly did. She was as sure of that as she was that when she learned the identity of the rotten person who had stolen that portfolio from her, she would kick her. *Hard.*

Her smile widened. "No trouble," she answered. "I was just thinking, that's all."

"You almost done here?"

She almost never saw Patrick two nights in the same week. Her willpower wasn't strong enough for that.

But she was tired and depressed. Very depressed. Too depressed to tell him she was too busy to see him, when, in fact, that was *exactly* what she wanted.

"Another hour," she said. "Why? Got something in mind?"

He grinned. "This is a public place. I can't tell you what I have in mind."

"Patrick, you're *leering*. But if you think you can behave yourself, I'll meet you after work."

He moved closer and called up in a low voice, "If I behave myself, we won't have any fun!"

She laughed. "Patrick," she said, feeling better already, "you do know how to cheer me up, don't you? I'll meet you at the main entrance in an hour."

"Right." He threw her a kiss, and left.

Portfolio or not, life seemed just a little less grim. For the first time that day, she smiled at the shoppers passing by, and a woman in a tan raincoat remarked to her husband, "Look at that. Isn't she just about the prettiest thing you've ever seen?"

Mary Ellen heard her, and widened her smile.

At Walt Manners' log-and-glass house in the woods, Olivia slammed shut the book they'd been studying and said, "Walt, how about if we call Angie and see if she'd like to go to the movies with us? I think she could use some cheering up."

"Sure," Walt said heartily, clearing books and papers from the dining room table. "Good idea. This will be the first Saturday night in a long time she hasn't been with Arne. She'll probably be kind of lonely."

But when Olivia hung up after calling Angie, her pretty oval face wore frown lines.

"She has a *date*," she announcd, turning away from the phone.

Walt looked up from his seat on the floor in front of the stone fireplace. "A date? Well, good for Arne! Didn't take him long to find out that computers are no substitute for a pretty girl."

Olivia shook her light brown hair vigorously. "No," she said slowly, joining him on the floor, "it's not with Arne. That's the funny thing." Folding her legs, clad in brown wool trousers, underneath her, she added, "She's not going out with Arne."

Walt put an arm around her shoulders. "Well, who is it, then?"

"I don't know." Olivia leaned against him, her orange sweater clashing violently with his cranberry turtleneck. "I asked her. She said it wasn't anyone we knew."

Looking down at her in surprise, Walt said, "How can it be someone we don't know? We know all the same people she does!"

"I know."

They were both quiet for a few minutes. Then Olivia added, "She just sounded so much better, I didn't want to spoil it by asking her a lot of questions. But I wonder who she's going out with."

"Don't know," Walt murmured. "But," he said in a cheerful voice, "I'm glad for Angie. And to tell you the truth, I'm glad for *us*. Now I'll have you all to myself."

"Walt!" she scolded, laughing. "You know you'd do anything to cheer up Angie if she really needed it."

"Ah, but she doesn't," he declared happily. "So whoever the guy is who's taking her out,

I'm grateful." And he bent his head and kissed her.

Then he jumped up, grabbed her hand, and pulled her to her feet. "C'mon, let's go see that movie!"

Helping her with her jacket, he added, "Maybe we'll run into Angie and her date. Then the mystery will be solved."

All the way into town in the Jeep, they speculated on who Angie's date might be.

Angie's date, in a dark brown suit, crisp white shirt, and beige tie, was driving the blue compact car down Main Street with Angie at his side. He had slicked his blond hair down flat against his head, which she had noticed with gratitude when she answered the door earlier. When it stuck straight up in the air, it reminded her too much of Arne.

But she was uncomfortable, in spite of his new hairstyle. Why was he so dressed up? Nobody in Tarenton wore suits on Saturday nights unless there was a prom. And they didn't even have any plans. They were just going to drive around town, maybe get something to eat. That's what he'd told her.

Compared to what he was wearing, the black wool pants and red cowl-neck sweater she often wore on Saturday nights seemed sloppy.

Maybe he was just trying to look professional. After all, this was kind of a business meeting.

They were supposed to "get to know each other" before the picture-taking began.

But did he need a suit for that?

"And that's the public library," she said, pointing toward a huge stone building, dark now. "And on the other side of the street is the post office, in case you need to mail anything. And that's the supermarket and there's a gas station on that corner and why did Mary Ellen turn you down?"

"What?"

"Oh, I'm sorry," Angie apologized as Reese pulled the car over to the curb and parked. "I didn't mean to blurt it out like that. But it's been driving me crazy! You're looking for a model and Mary Ellen Kirkwood is the prettiest girl in town. Everybody thinks so. So why isn't she posing for you instead of me?"

"I'm not everybody," he said cryptically, which told her nothing.

"Well," she pressed on, "you said you had talked to two of the cheerleaders. I can guess which two. Mary Ellen and Nancy Goldstein, right?"

"Right."

"Well, I need to know why you picked me instead of them. Or did they both just say they didn't want to do it?"

"Nancy said no. Said she wasn't interested."

Angie nodded. That was no surprise. "But Mary Ellen?"

"I told you before," he said patiently, turning to face her on the front seat. "Neither one of them was the right type. *You're* the right type."

"You mean *you* turned Mary Ellen down?"

He thought for a moment before answering. Then, "Yeah, I guess I did," he said.

She groaned.

"At first she said she didn't think she'd have the time. She didn't seem all that interested. I think she was suspicious."

"Of *you*?"

"Yeah. I mean, I gave her my card, but I could tell she wasn't sure I was for real."

"Well, that's just plain silly!" Angie said indignantly. "Why would you lie?"

He shrugged. A neon restaurant sign above them flicked on and off, casting red and blue stripes across his face. "People *do* lie, Angie. All the time. I figure she probably went home and checked *American Sports* magazine to see if my name was in it."

"Is it?"

"Oh, yeah," he said casually. "Then she called me back to say she'd do it. But I'd seen you by then. And like I told you, I knew right away that you were perfect."

"And you told her that?"

"I didn't tell her who you were. I just said I'd found somebody else."

Poor Mary Ellen! "Was she upset?"

"I guess. But it doesn't matter. You're the best model for the pictures, and that's all there is to it."

Angie felt terrible, remembering her thoughts

about Mary Ellen "just dying" when she found out about all of this. But that had been when she'd thought Mary Ellen had turned *him* down. And she hadn't really mean't it, anyway.

What would happen when Mary Ellen found out it was her friend Angie Poletti that Reese Oliver was photographing instead of her?

What would it do to the squad?

"Well," she said with a little shudder, "you were right about not telling my friends about this. The more time I have before they know, the better off I am." She frowned. "They might end up taking sides, like they did once before when Mary Ellen and I had a problem, and things got really messy on the squad."

"I'm shocked," he said, and she sensed a smile on his red-and-blue face. "I didn't think cheerleaders ever fought. I mean, it doesn't go with the image, does it?"

"What image?" she asked, puzzled.

"Oh, you know . . . the great American cheerleader, straight-A student, pillar of the community, smiling and cheerful at all times."

"We're not like that," she said slowly. "We're not like that at all. Is that what you think?"

"Oh, it's not what *I* think. I just mean that's the image. I guess I was wrong."

A little unsettled, she changed the subject by asking, "I don't see how I can give you a tour of Tarenton without anybody seeing us, do you? It's Saturday night. Everyone will be out. Most of the people here know who I am, and *none* of them knows who you are. In a small town, that's all it takes for the gossip to get going."

"No problem. You're already *giving* me the tour. When we get hungry, we'll just hit one of those places on the highway outside of town. No one needs to see us at all. I can see Tarenton just fine from the car.

"Anyway," he added, putting the car in gear and pulling away from the curb, "what I really need to do tonight is get to know *you*, not the town. We can do that while we drive. So start with the day you were born and go on from there."

Trying to ignore her worry about Mary Ellen, and trying to ignore Reese's unsettling comments about cheerleaders, Angie began talking.

Just a short distance away, in the cab of a garbage truck, Patrick was also talking. He was telling Mary Ellen to quit worrying about the photographer who got away.

"Sounds like a phony to me," he said, taking a sharp corner with calm efficiency. "How many good photographers travel across the country, drumming up business? Sounds like weirdsville to me."

"I *told* you," Mary Ellen said impatiently, "I saw his name right there in the magazine, for Pete's sake! Don't you believe me?"

"It's not *you* I don't believe," he said bluntly, pulling the truck into a space in front of a restaurant. "I'm sure you saw the name. I'm just not convinced that it belongs to the guy you met."

"Oh, Patrick, that's ridiculous! Why would he use someone else's name?"

Patrick glanced over at her, his head tilted to one side. "Are you kidding? To get what he wants. From you. It's been done before."

She shook her head. "No. It wasn't like that. *He* wasn't like that. He was very professional. You should have seen the camera equipment he had."

"*I* have camera equipment. But that doesn't make me a professional photographer."

"Listen, Patrick," she said firmly, "after hanging around *you* all this time, nobody knows better than I the signs of a guy who has plans for me that my parents wouldn't like."

Patrick moved closer. "Oh, yeah?" he asked softly. "You mean like this?" He put his arm around her and lifted her chin.

His kiss was strong and warm and as she closed her eyes and fit her arms around his neck, she shoved all thoughts of Reese Oliver and his camera into a tiny closet in her mind, and closed and locked the door. They could come out later, maybe, when she was somewhere other than in Patrick Henley's arms.

But as his arms tightened and his kisses became more intense, Mary Ellen tensed.

She moved away from him. "You promised to feed me, and I'm starving to death. You also promised me a movie, remember?"

"Movies are bad for your eyes," he said, keeping his arm right where it was. "I heard it on the news."

"Oh, yeah? Well, I heard that sitting in a truck with a guy's arm around you and a gleam in his eye is bad for a girl's health. Now, come on, feed me like you promised!"

He groaned. But he got out of the truck and followed her into the pizza place.

CHAPTER

When Mary Ellen and Patrick came out of the theater later, they spotted Walt, Olivia, and Pres just ahead of them. And Vanessa, wearing the black satin pants Mary Ellen had modeled that afternoon. On her arm was a tall, broad-shouldered blond guy with a stupid but adoring expression on his face. Vanessa preferred the obedient, slow-minded type. If I walked up to him and asked him his name, Mary Ellen thought with scorn, he'd have to stop and think before giving me an answer. She searched Vanessa's face for some sign of triumph or excitement and found no more than she had that afternoon. There was nothing in that thin, foxlike face to suggest that Vanessa was harboring a terrific secret.

"Pizza?" Walt called out eagerly, as Mary Ellen and Patrick joined the three cheerleaders.

Mary Ellen groaned. "I've already had my quota today. How about a hamburger instead?"

"What do you think?" Walt asked with a broad grin. "It's *food,* isn't it?"

When they were settled in a booth at the restaurant, Mary Ellen said, "Too bad Angie isn't here. She would have liked the movie. Might have cheered her up."

"She had a date," Olivia said, watching Mary Ellen's face. She got the reaction she expected.

"What? A date? Who with? Don't tell me Arne came out of his fog!"

Olivia shook her head. Everyone in the booth listened, curious about Angie's date.

"Wasn't Arne," she said. "Angie would have said so. And she wasn't all that excited about it, the way she would have been if it had been Arne."

"Well, *who* then?" Mary Ellen asked as the waitress plunked their hamburgers down on the table.

"Vic Stainbrook has had his eye on her for a long time," Walt said, before taking a huge bite of his sandwich.

"So has Andy Passenger," Pres said. "He talks about her all the time."

Olivia swallowed a bite of her sandwich before shaking her head again. "She said it wasn't anyone we knew."

"Well, that's silly!" Mary Ellen said. "*We* know everyone *she* knows. Maybe the guy is a well-known nerd and she's too embarrassed to tell you."

"That's dumb," Pres said, brushing a lock of dark blond hair back from his forehead. "Angie doesn't have to date nerds. There are lots of guys at school who think she's cute."

"Including you?" Mary Ellen teased. She knew he was between girls. She also knew he was getting restless.

But Pres shook his head. He'd tried the wholesome, unsophisticated type when he dated Kerry Elliott. It hadn't worked. He couldn't be something he wasn't.

"Well, *we* know Angie doesn't have to date nerds," Olivia agreed. "The trouble is, *she* doesn't know it. Not right now, anyway."

"We could always fix her up with someone," Walt suggested.

"Oh, no," Mary Ellen said emphatically. "She'd hate that! She'd die if she found out."

"Mary Ellen's right," Pres agreed. "Anyway, what are we worrying about? Olivia said Angie *has* a date tonight. It's not like she's sitting at home counting the cracks in the ceiling."

"There aren't any cracks in her ceiling," Walt said, grinning. "She doesn't live in a big, ancient mansion like you, Pres. The Poletti house is fairly new."

His teasing lightened their mood, and they changed the subject, leaving Angie's love life to straighten itself out.

Angie wasn't thinking about her love life. Reese had already seen everything in Tarenton and she was glad the tour was over. Growing up with it all of her life had taken the excitement out of the evening for her.

If she had been one of those people who loved to talk about themselves, she would have had a wonderful time. Reese hadn't asked her much about Tarenton, but his string of questions about herself had seemed endless. He asked her questions she had no answers to because she'd never thought about them.

"Reese," she said finally, "you're not going to write a book about me. You're just going to take my picture!"

"Taking pictures of someone *is* writing a book," he said mildly. "Haven't you ever heard the expression, 'One picture is worth a thousand words'?"

She said she had.

"Well, that won't work unless you know your subject. I'm sorry if I gave you the third degree, but I told you I needed to get to know you."

But he finally took her home and after she'd thanked him and hurried inside, it occurred to her that it was a good thing she wasn't taking *his* picture. Because although she'd spent the entire evening with him, the only thing she'd learned about him was that he asked more questions than a Trivial Pursuit game.

She didn't even know if he had a girl.

Deciding that it really wasn't important, she went into the kitchen to see what her mother had baked while she was gone.

* * *

Mary Ellen and Patrick stood on the little cement stoop outside the Kirkwoods' turquoise house.

"Thanks for feeding me," she said, leaning into Patrick's navy blue down jacket, "and thanks for the movie."

"Yeah," Patrick said softly into her hair, "I just wish you'd let me do it more often."

She lifted her head. "Patrick, you know how hectic my schedule is. There's cheerleading and keeping my grades up and my job — "

"Cut it out, Mary Ellen," he said, putting one hand under her chin. "We both know why Olivia and Walt, and Nancy and Ben have something we don't."

In her head, she saw a pair of white coveralls doing a little dance, tormenting her. There wasn't any point in denying it. Patrick understood her too well.

"It's okay," he said quietly. "I haven't given up. If I had, I wouldn't be standing here, would I?"

They stood close together, silently, for a long while before saying good-night with one last, clinging kiss.

Mary Ellen wondered, as she did so often, if she was making a horrible mistake by choosing New York City and a modeling career over Tarenton and sweet, strong, sexy Patrick.

She sat by her window for a long time, looking out into the darkness, before going to bed.

* * *

Angie, not trusting herself to keep quiet about Reese Oliver, avoided the other cheerleaders until practice on Monday afternoon. She purposely arrived late to escape locker room chatter, and out on the floor, she concentrated totally on the new routine they were learning. A trick number relying heavily on gymnastics, it required perfect timing on her part to do a back arch, two toe touches, and the final double cartwheel.

She had no mental energy left for Reese Oliver or Mary Ellen.

"Well done!" Ardith cried, applauding as they finished, perfectly synchronized. Giving Angie a pat on the shoulder, she said heartily, "Atta girl! Glad to see you back in fine form again. Keep it up, okay?"

"I'll try," Angie said with a grin.

In the locker room, she turned off the shower just as Nancy called to Mary Ellen, "Hey, Melon, I forgot to tell you . . . the other night at the mall this weird guy stopped me in the parking lot and wanted to take my picture. Can you believe it?"

Angie's hand stopped in midair on its way back from the shower dial.

"In the mall?" Mary Ellen called in a voice that sounded strange to Angie. Like she had something caught in her throat.

"Yeah. In the parking lot. Just walked right up to me and said something about me making a great model. Even had a business card."

All three girls, wrapped in towels, emerged

from their showers at the same time, to join Olivia at the long mirror over the sinks.

"What was his name?" Mary Ellen asked in that same strange voice.

"I don't remember. Reed, or something like that. He looked like a very tall rabbit."

Angie studied the floor tiles. Olivia turned on her hair dryer. Mary Ellen stood quietly, her eyes on Nancy's face. Her own was very pale.

Mary Ellen was thinking that she would almost prefer that it had been Vanessa rather than Nancy. Nancy Goldstein with her perfectly polished nails, her perfectly arranged hairstyles, her perfectly coordinated wardrobe. Nancy with her Brooke Shields eyes and her well-ordered life. She didn't want it to be Nancy.

"And you said yes," Mary Ellen said.

Nancy stared at her. "Are you nuts? The guy was obviously a phony! I mean, professional photographers don't run around in parking lots looking for clients. Do they?"

Angie's cheeks burned and she hid her head under a towel on the pretext of rubbing her hair dry.

The color flooded back into Mary Ellen's face. Nancy had refused to model for Reese Oliver. Her relief was so great, it made her eyes water.

"That's exactly what Patrick said!" Mary Ellen cried.

Nancy frowned. "Patrick? I didn't tell Patrick. I haven't even seen him."

Angie came out from under the towel. She

needed to see faces during this conversation. She hated every single word of it, but hiding wouldn't do any good.

"No, no," Mary Ellen said quickly. "*I* told Patrick. The same guy talked to me in the mall. He said he'd do a model's portfolio for me."

Nancy's eyes widened. "He *did*? You must have turned him down or he wouldn't have approached me, would he? Or is he looking for a whole bunch of models? I can't believe you turned him down."

If I turn on my hair drier, Angie thought, I won't hear any more of this horrible conversation. But didn't she need to know what Mary Ellen was thinking?

"Well," Mary Ellen said honestly, "I didn't exactly turn him down." She began braiding her damp hair, so familiar with the task that she needed no mirror. "I wanted to check him out, so I said I'd let him know."

So far, Angie thought, they haven't really said anything about Reese that I didn't already know. And they haven't said anything really bad.

"By the time I called him back at his motel," Mary Ellen continued, still braiding, "he'd found somebody else. Boy, was I upset! At first, I thought it was probably Vanessa."

"Yuk!" Olivia said, dressed and ready to go, but too interested in the conversation to leave.

"If he's found somebody," Nancy said, "it could be Vanessa. She's not stupid, but she's vain enough to fall for the idea."

71

Angie winced. She was suddenly terribly grateful that Reese had warned her against telling the others. Hadn't Nancy just called her stupid? She just didn't know that it was Angie she was talking about.

"No, it's not Vanessa," Mary Ellen said. "At least, I'm pretty sure it isn't. She was in the mall on Saturday and I know she would have made sure I knew she was posing for some big, professional photographer. But she never said a word about it. She said she was bored."

"Then who *is* it?" Olivia asked.

Mary Ellen shook her head. "I don't know. I even thought it might be you, Nancy."

Nancy, halfway into a pale yellow cashmere sweater, called out in a muffled voice, "Oh, please! Give me some credit for brains." Her head emerged from the soft sweater. "You said you checked him out. How?"

Angie held her breath.

Mary Ellen finished braiding. "He said he'd done some work for *American Sports* magazine. My dad had a copy at home so I looked inside, and sure enough, his name was in there."

Angie smiled, but no one noticed.

Nancy zipped her yellow plaid skirt. "Big deal," she said, turning toward the mirror to push her hair into place. "That doesn't prove anything. He could have seen the name in the magazine just like you did, and borrowed it."

I always thought Mary Ellen was the cynical one, Angie thought with surprise. But Nancy makes Mary Ellen look like Pollyanna!

Mary Ellen stepped into her jeans and yanked them upward. "But do you really think he went out and made up a bunch of business cards with someone else's name on them? Isn't that illegal or something?"

Nancy shrugged and carefully applied lip gloss before answering. "I don't know. All I do know is, I thought the whole thing was really weird, this guy coming up to me in the parking lot." Then she faced Mary Ellen with new respect in her eyes. "And I'm glad you didn't get mixed up with him, either. But I still can't believe you turned down a chance to be photographed."

Still not as convinced as Nancy that Reese was a phony, Mary Ellen buttoned her navy blue blouse and said gloomily, "Well, I really didn't have the chance, did I? He who hesitates is lost, and I hesitated. So I lost. And to tell you the truth," she added, pulling on her boots, "I'm dying to know who won."

"Oh, Mary Ellen," Nancy said impatiently, picking up her books, "you did the right thing. I'm sure of it. The whole thing was just too weird."

"Maybe. But there are probably lots of modeling agencies that send photographers out around the country looking for models. Sort of like a giant talent search. He seemed nice enough to me, and besides, nobody would carry all that camera equipment around just for show. He *must* know how to use it."

"Lots of people know how to use cameras. They don't run around parking lots looking for models."

Angie, remembering Reese's warning, fought the temptation to talk to Mary Ellen about him, and left.

When Mary Ellen turned around and discovered that Angie wasn't there, she said in disgust, "Nancy, we never even asked Angie who she went out with Saturday night!"

"Well, it couldn't have been anybody terrific," Nancy said matter-of-factly, "or she would have been bursting to tell us. I thought she was awfully quiet today, didn't you?"

"Yeah. She certainly wasn't the picture of a girl with a new love. So it couldn't have been Prince Charming."

Angie, driving home, was a lot more upset about Patrick's judgment of Reese than she was about Nancy's. She trusted Patrick. He'd been a good friend to her.

But Patrick was, after all, just an ordinary person. And he could be wrong, just like any ordinary person.

And this time, he was. She was sure of it.

CHAPTER

When Reese dropped by the Poletti house later in the day, minus camera equipment, Angie said lightly as she led him into the den, "Reese, aren't you ready to start taking pictures yet? After that grilling you gave me the other night, you know more about me than my own mother knows!"

He flopped into a chair and frowned up at her. At least, she thought, sitting down on the couch, he's not wearing a suit tonight. The plaid flannel shirt and jeans reminded her of Pres, since that was the sort of thing he wore all the time. And he had slicked his hair down again, the way Pres did.

But he still doesn't look anything like him, she thought firmly. They're as different as night and day. Even though Reese was older and a professional, he didn't seem nearly as self-confident and arrogant as Pres.

"Look, Angie," he said, staring at her from under bushy reddish eyebrows, "you're the model. *I'm* the photographer, and I decide when we're ready to shoot, okay?"

"Well, sure. I just thought — "

"Well, *don't* think! If there's one thing a photographer can't stand, it's a thinking model. They're too much trouble."

She didn't believe that for a second. It made no sense. A stupid model would be far more difficult to work with than a smart one. The photographer would say, "Turn to your right," and the model would say, "Where is it?" *That* certainly wouldn't be any fun for the person taking the pictures.

But she didn't argue with him. It struck her as ironic that Arne had complained that she didn't think enough, that she needed to develop what he called her "powers of reasoning." Now here was Reese telling her to skip the brain games and let someone else use their gray matter *for* her.

"By the way," he said casually, "I'm going to need an advance on my fee. Have to buy some equipment, and I'm going to check around for a studio we can use, a loft or something with good light. We'll only need it for a couple of afternoons. There must be something like that in town somewhere."

She didn't know of any place, and said so.

He shrugged. "I'll check around. I'm not real

keen on taking pictures in a motel room. The light in there stinks, for one thing. And it doesn't look very professional, for another. I'll see what I can find. But I need some bucks."

"I'll take some money out of my savings account tomorrow," Angie said. After all, it wouldn't be fair to make *him* pay the tab when it was *her* modeling career they were trying to establish.

Later, she tried asking him questions about himself, but it was like trying to dig a hole in a brick. He was an absolute genius at evading her questions.

When she asked him where he went to school, he said, "What makes you think I went to school?" — the first time she'd seen him attempt any humor at all.

"Everybody goes to school."

He shook his head. "Not everybody. There are any number of cultures on this planet that get their entire education in the home or from the elders in their villages."

When she asked him where he was from, she got another shrug and, "All over. My dad was in the Army. We moved around a lot."

In one last feeble effort to learn something about Reese Oliver, she said in a deliberately casual tone of voice, "There's a football game on television if you're interested in sports."

He said simply, "The only game worth paying any attention to at all is basketball."

Which told her only that he liked basketball.

She had to admire the way he refused to reveal anything about himself. None of it was probably important, anyway, as long as he took good pictures. Being private was a talent she herself had never possessed, and she knew it.

But I can always learn, she thought with determination. And this is probably the perfect time to start, since I know something about me now I don't want to share with the squad just yet.

So the next day at their warm-up practice session before the game with Summerville, when Olivia asked Angie who her Saturday night date had been, she shrugged the same way Reese had, and answered, "Nobody you know." Then she ran out onto the floor to practice her cartwheels.

"Well, that was really weird!" Olivia said in a low voice. Mary Ellen and Nancy, standing close enough to hear the exchange, nodded.

"It sure was," Mary Ellen agreed.

"Frankly," Nancy said, "I think she's been acting funny ever since she and Arne split up. And I think we should find out *why*."

"Well," Olivia said between stretches, "it really isn't any of our business who she's dating, is it?"

"Oh, yes it is!" Mary Ellen said. She looked beautiful, her pale hair in a thick, curly ponytail, her fair skin glowing with excitement as it aways did before a game. "It's our business because if she's in any kind of trouble it'll affect her performance here."

Olivia frowned. "Trouble? Who said anything about trouble?"

Mary Ellen shook her head. "It's just a feeling I have, okay? It's not like Angie to hide things. She always tells us everything. She was really feeling bad about Arne splitting up with her, and maybe she's turned to some jerk. She is definitely hiding something."

They all stood there watching Angie's strong, athletic body flip through the air with as little effort as she used to tie a shoe.

The Summerville Patriots were in fine form. But the Tarenton Wolves, headed by their captain, Donny Parish, swallowed the Patriots whole, thanks to some stunning baskets sent like lightning bolts into the net from the hands of Ben Adamson.

Nancy, excited for Ben and for herself, screamed herself hoarse and couldn't wait until he took her home after the game and she could show him how proud she was of his performance.

As happy as Mary Ellen was with the win, she ran off the floor frowning. But she said nothing to anyone until Angie, saying she had to go straight home to study for a test, left with the Eismar twins.

Then Mary Ellen gathered the other cheerleaders together in the hall outside the locker room.

"What's up?" Walt asked her. "My taste buds are salivating for pizza. Did we do something wrong tonight?"

"No, no," Mary Ellen assured him, shaking her head. "We were great tonight." They *had* been, and she stopped for a moment to imagine how they must have looked on the floor, executing their routines with precision and enthusiasm, their red-and-white uniforms a whirling circle of color.

Then she remembered what she wanted from them. "Forget the pizza!" she commanded sharply. "Something's going on with Angie and we need to find out what it is."

"Why?" Pres asked, leaning against the wall, hands in the pockets of his jeans. "She was fine tonight. She zipped through the new routines as if she'd been doing them all her life. So what's the problem?"

"The problem," Mary Ellen said firmly, just as Ben came up behind Nancy and put his arms around her waist, "is that she hardly said a word to any of us all night long. Didn't you notice?"

"I did." This from Nancy, after she'd reached up to give Ben a quick kiss of congratulations.

"Yeah," Pres said mildly, "but we're not out there to talk. We're out there to cheer, and Angie did just fine in that department."

"I agree," Mary Ellen persisted, "but there's something going on with her, something she's keeping from us. And if there's one thing I've learned on this squad, it's that letting problems go when they first come up makes them ten times worse in the long run. I say we go over to her house now and talk to her."

Ben gave Nancy a look of warning. "C'mon, Nance," he said, "I thought we were gonna have some time alone. It's Mary Ellen's idea, let *her*

80

go and you come with me." He grinned. "I'm perfectly willing to share my secrets with you."

Nancy looked definitely interested. But she shook her head. "No, Ben, I'm sorry. It involves the whole squad, so I'm included. Come with us, though, and you can take me home afterwards."

Grumbling under his breath, Ben reluctantly agreed.

So did the others, although Pres repeated once more that as long as Angie was performing well, what difference did it make whether or not she talked to anyone?

Dividing into Ben's Isuzu, Walt's Jeep, and Pres's Porsche, they drove to the Poletti house.

"Hey, she's got company," Walt announced as they pulled into the driveway. "That's not the Poletti car," referring to the compact car parked just outside the garage.

"Probably somebody visiting her mother," Olivia said.

They all piled out of the cars and walked through the darkness to the front door.

Angie answered the door. Mary Ellen, standing just ahead of the others, watched her eyes widen.

"What — what are you doing here?" She held the door open slightly.

"We came over to cheer you up," Mary Ellen said brightly.

"Cheer me up? Why?"

"Well, you were so quiet tonight," Mary Ellen answered, glancing around at the others for confirmation. Nancy and Olivia nodded.

Angie frowned. "Was there something wrong with my cheerleading?"

"No, of course not! You were great!" From the rear of the group, Mary Ellen heard Pres mutter, "See? I knew she'd think that!"

"Well, can we come in?" Nancy asked. "It's cold out here."

"Oh. Well. . . ." Angie glanced behind her and then back at Mary Ellen. Reese was safely inside the den, with the door closed. If she could just get them all into the kitchen. . . .

She was just not hardhearted enough to say, Go away. I don't want you here. Besides, it was clear that Mary Ellen was determined.

So she stood back, pulled the door open, and let them all in. "There's soda in the kitchen if you're thirsty. Go help yourselves." I'll give them all something to drink in the kitchen, she decided, and then think of an excuse to get them out of the house. A headache . . . a sudden case of the plague . . . maybe I'll just scream, *Fire!*

When they were all inside, she closed the door and turned to follow them into the kitchen, to find Reese Oliver standing in the doorway to the den.

Mary Ellen and Nancy, in the hall, stared at him in amazement.

CHAPTER

There was a long, awkward pause. Nancy, Mary Ellen, and Angie stood perfectly still. Walt and Pres, almost to the kitchen, stopped and turned around, then walked back to join the girls.

"Oh, hi," Walt said innocently, stepping forward and extending his hand. "I'm Walt Manners."

Angie sighed heavily and, avoiding Mary Ellen's eyes, moved over beside Reese as he shook Walt's hand.

"Everybody," she said with a cheerfulness she didn't feel, "this is . . . a friend of mine, Reese Oliver." She went through the group quickly, telling Reese everyone's name as he nodded and said, "Hi."

When the introductions were finished, there was another awkward pause.

Then Mary Ellen said in a thin, high voice, "Angie, why don't the girls all go get the soda? The guys can wait in the den."

Pres laughed. "Boy, that's a switch! You mean you liberated females are actually going to wait on us guys?"

"Now that's more like it," Ben added heartily, grinning at Nancy. "I love being waited on!"

"Well, you've got it," Mary Ellen said in that same high voice. "So go on in and sit down. Angie?"

Reluctantly, Angie trailed along behind the girls as Reese and the other boys disappeared into the den.

In the kitchen, Mary Ellen pushed the swinging door shut when they were all inside and whirled to face Angie.

"What is *he* doing here?" she whispered, her agitation making the whisper louder than she'd intended.

Angie, thinking fast, decided to try Reese's approach to questions again. Shrugging and turning away toward the refrigerator, she said vaguely, "Visiting."

"Visiting?" Mary Ellen's cheeks matched her scarlet sweater. "I didn't even know you *knew* him!"

"Oh, sure." She wouldn't volunteer any information unless she absolutely had to.

"Where did you meet him?" Nancy asked, as Angie took out several bottles of soda and placed them on the counter.

Before Angie could answer, Olivia said, "Please, would someone just tell me what's going on here? Who *is* that guy, anyway?"

"His name is Reese Oliver," Angie said calmly, pouring soda into glasses sitting on a red plastic tray.

"I *know* that much!" Olivia hissed. "I was listening when you introduced him. But *who* is he? What's he doing here?"

"He's a traveling salesman," Nancy said curtly, watching Angie's face.

"He is *not!*" Whirling to face Nancy, Angie said hotly, "He's a professional photographer and he's going to do a model's portfolio for me. He said I'm just right for the magazine market today."

There was a very long moment of shocked silence, during which Angie didn't have the courage to look at Mary Ellen. Instead, she carefully studied the glasses, as if checking to see if the soda had somehow escaped when she wasn't looking.

Then Mary Ellen laughed. "Of *you?*" she asked, staring at Angie, forcing her to look up. "He's going to do *your* portfolio?"

Angie's face felt as if someone was holding a torch under her chin. "Yes," she said defiantly, "he is."

Olivia, putting chips into a bowl from the bag Angie had handed her, said warmly, "Gee, Angie, that's exciting! I never knew you were interested in modeling. I always thought it was Mary Ellen who — " She stopped talking to look at Mary Ellen's face. It was ashen. Olivia swallowed hard. She had no idea exactly what was going on, but it was obvious that it wasn't good.

"I don't believe it," Mary Ellen said softly. "It *can't* be you!"

"You mean," Angie said in a shaky voice, "that no photographer in his right mind would use plain old me as a model, right? Especially when he could have you. Or Nancy. Even Vanessa would be better than me, right, Mary Ellen?"

That was so close to what Mary Ellen was thinking that it set her teeth on edge. She said nothing, because her mind wasn't working properly. It was still reeling in shock.

"Angie," Nancy asked, "are you sure this guy is for real? I mean, how do you know he's who he says he is?"

Suddenly remembering a remark she'd overheard Mary Ellen make to Nancy, Angie said, "I'll prove to you that he's really a photographer, okay? Then maybe you'll leave me alone. Wait right here!"

She ran out of the room and was back in seconds, waving a magazine in the air. "This is Andrew's," she said, flipping through the pages while they all watched. "I knew he had it, so I borrowed it to show you you're wrong."

Finding what she was looking for, she thrust the open magazine under Nancy's nose, saying triumphantly, "There! Read that! What does it say?"

Nancy read aloud, "Reese Oliver. It's in the list

of photographic credits. But that doesn't really prove anything, Angie."

"Oh, honestly!" Angie said in disgust. "Well, I guess I shouldn't be surprised." She handed the magazine to Olivia. "Reese said you'd be jealous. And he was right."

"Jealous?" Nancy screeched. "Why would I be jealous? I had a chance to model for him, and I turned him down!"

"Mary Ellen didn't," Angie pointed out. "She'd be modeling for him right now if he hadn't asked me instead."

Mary Ellen looked up as if she just remembered where she was. "She's right," she said in a lifeless voice. "I was all ready to tell him I'd do it."

Olivia tried desperately to think of some way to make things right, and failed.

"Reese has been very professional," Angie said, looking at Nancy. "He hasn't done anything to make me suspect that he's not who he says he is."

Nancy groaned. "All I can say is," she threw over her shoulder as she walked out of the room, "I hope you do more checking before you hand the guy any money." Then she pushed through the swinging doors and was gone.

Angie bit her lip, her flush deepening. She had given Reese the promised advance just five minutes before the others arrived.

"Hey, where are those drinks?" Pres yelled from the den.

Olivia picked up the tray of glasses. Still uncertain about what was going on and feeling totally useless, she decided to leave Angie and Mary Ellen alone.

"See you inside," she said, and made her exit.

When she had gone, Angie said quietly, "We'd better go in, too. We're not accomplishing anything out here. I'm sorry you're disappointed. But you'll have lots of chances to model, and this is a chance I never expected to have. And," she added, her voice harsh, "you obviously don't think I should even have this one."

Mary Ellen shook her head slowly. "No, I never said that. I'm glad for you. Honest." But there was no feeling in her voice, and her eyes didn't meet Angie's.

"Yeah, right," Angie said. "Nancy thinks I'm stupid and naive, and you think any photographer who would want to take my picture is either blind or crazy. Well, I want to do this. And I'm going to. I just wish you and Nancy would give him a chance."

She turned on her heels and walked out of the kitchen, her steps more determined than she felt inside.

After a few minutes, Mary Ellen followed. But her own steps were slow and sluggish, her lovely face grim. It *was* Angie. She couldn't believe it. A professional photographer thought Angie Poletti would make a better model than Mary Ellen Kirkwood.

I can't deal with this, she thought as she

entered the crowded den. I can't deal with this at all.

And even seeing Patrick sitting beside Walt on the floor in front of the television set did nothing to change the expression on her face. Still stunned, she stared right through Patrick as if he was invisible.

The look on her face brought him to his feet. He was at her side in seconds, climbing over people on the floor to get to her. Taking her elbow, he pulled her gently out of the room.

In the hall, he asked, "What's wrong?" as she stared at him with dull eyes.

"Oh, hi, Patrick," she answered, her voice lifeless. "I didn't know you were here."

"I was at the gas station up the street when the Jeep went by. I figured you were coming here. Didn't think you'd mind if I dropped in. What's wrong?"

"What? Oh, nothing. Nothing. Anyway, why would *I* mind if you showed up? It's not my house, is it? It's Angie's." Then she added bitterly, "Angie can have anyone she wants in her own house, can't she?"

And she turned and went back into the den, leaving him completely mystified.

Mary Ellen's depression deepened when she saw how well Reese was getting along with the other guys. He wasn't saying much, but he was listening to Walt, Pres, and Ben discussing the game, and he seemed interested. It looked very much like Nancy Goldstein was the only person in the room suspicious of Reese.

And me? she wondered as Patrick came up behind her and put his hands on her shoulders. Do I think he's a phony, too? And the depressing answer came quickly: No. I *want* to believe he's not really a photographer, she thought sadly, but I don't. His name *is* in that magazine. And Angie knows him better than anyone and she trusts him. And I trust her!

She looked up at Patrick with tears in her eyes.

"Let's get out of here," he said brusquely. Without waiting for an answer from her, he called to the others, "Hey, guys, we're going to split. See you tomorrow."

"Mary Ellen, wait!" Angie called, but Mary Ellen kept walking. Because if she turned around, Angie would see the losing battle she was waging against tears.

But Angie caught up with them at the door. "Mary Ellen, please. . . ."

Mary Ellen swiped at her eyes with one hand and turned. "It's okay, Angie. Really." Then she just couldn't talk anymore. She turned and hurried out of the house.

As Angie, misery written across her face, stared after Mary Ellen, Patrick said, "What's going *on*?"

Angie shook her head. "She'll tell you," she said. "Maybe you can make her feel better."

"Well, I'll give it a shot," Patrick replied doubtfuly. He hadn't an inkling about why Mary Ellen was so upset. She was obviously hurting and he wasn't at all sure he could help.

He didn't even try during the drive to her house. She sat quietly beside him, her hands folded in her lap, and he didn't question her. As much as he wanted to know what she was thinking, he was willing to wait for her to tell him.

What Mary Ellen was thinking was that she'd been a total fool. All those big ideas about going off to New York City and knocking the modeling world off its feet! How could I have been so stupid? she asked herself angrily, biting her lip. If I were really that gorgeous, Reese would have waited for my answer. He just wasn't all that interested.

This was the first time Mary Ellen had lost something, in spite of her good looks. The job at Marnie's had gone to Vanessa first only because of Mary Ellen's schedule. So that didn't count.

The thing that frightened her the most was the sickening realization that if she couldn't win over Angie Poletti, who was cute but certainly not beautiful, she didn't stand a chance in New York, a city crammed full of gorgeous girls from all over the country.

Finding out who Reese Oliver's new model was had been more humiliating than the time she'd fallen off Walt's shoulders and landed on the floor of a very crowded gym. It had been more painful than the car accident that sent her to the hospital.

And it was almost more frightening than the time Angie fell through the ice on the lake, because if Mary Ellen didn't have modeling, what did she have? Nothing, that's what!

She felt as if she was floundering in the middle of a huge ocean with no sign of land in any direction.

Patrick pulled up in front of the house and turned off the engine.

She sat there quietly for a few seconds. Then she turned and, without a word, threw her arms around his neck and hung on as if she was drowning and he was a life preserver.

Patrick, totally in the dark about what had happened, could easily have taken advantage of Mary Ellen's state of mind. It was obvious that she needed comforting. It was equally obvious that she wasn't her usual logical, practical self — the self that refused to become deeply involved with a trash collector.

Patrick, my boy, he told himself as Mary Ellen clung to him and he smelled the fresh lemony scent in her hair, if ever there was a time for your conscience to take a vacation, this is it.

But he knew he couldn't do it. Because for one thing, he wasn't at all sure that it was *him* Mary Ellen wanted right now. Maybe anyone who was willing to hold her and tell her everything would be okay would have filled the bill. And Patrick had pride. His father had instilled it in him, knowing that Patrick would need it, if he was to continue in the trash-collecting business and feel good about doing it. And it was Patrick's pride that made him want Mary Ellen to cling to him when she was happy, not when she was sad.

Besides, if she was hurting, an hour or two of heavy breathing wasn't going to help her. What she really needed was a shoulder to cry on. *That* he could give her.

"Mary Ellen," Patrick said, lifting her chin, "tell me what's wrong."

CHAPTER

When Mary Ellen had filled Patrick in on the details, he shook his head.

"Mary Ellen," he said as she rested her head on his chest, "any guy who picks someone else over you, even someone as cute and nice as Angie, has a brick loose in his chimney. Don't let it bother you. I told you, there's something weird about that guy."

"Nancy doesn't trust him," Mary Ellen agreed. She felt better already. There didn't seem to be anything that couldn't be helped by the wonderful feeling of having Patrick's arms around her. What was she going to use as a cure-all when he wasn't around anymore? She shuddered and turned to throw her arms around him again, giving him a kiss that left her toes weak.

"Whew!" Patrick said in a husky voice. "Did you just feel the truck shake? Take it easy. I'm only human. Listen," he added, "I'm the official school photographer, right? That means I know a little something about taking pictures. I'll take your picture any time you want. And it'll be free. Can't beat that, can you?"

She lifted her head to smile up at him. "You're wonderful, Patrick, you really are."

"Don't say things you don't mean, kiddo. You might regret it later."

"I *do* mean it, Patrick!"

He couldn't see her face in the darkness, but he didn't need to. He knew it by heart. He saw it all the time, awake and asleep. If he'd been an artist, he could have painted her portrait without even a photograph to guide him.

"Mary Ellen — " he began, but a finger on his lips silenced him.

"Shh!" she said, lifting her face. "You talk too much."

He laughed. But then he bent his head to kiss her. Who was he to argue?

She held onto him so tightly, his neck ached. And the kiss she gave him was so full of feeling, so full of warmth, that he responded fully. Even knowing that she couldn't possibly care as much as he did, didn't spoil the moment for him. For the first time, he knew what it would be like if Mary Ellen ever decided that they belonged together.

It made him dizzy.

And it almost made it impossible for him to pull away. He would rather have run two thousand laps at the track in a raging blizzard in his bare feet than separate from this warm and clinging Mary Ellen.

But the dizziness and the joy of the moment couldn't erase the thought that she was just reacting to the hurt and humiliation she'd suffered.

When Mary Ellen decided they belonged together, he wanted it to be because she'd made a choice. Not because she felt she *had* no choice.

He groaned. "Mary Ellen," he said from between clenched teeth, "I'm going to take you into your house now, where you'll be safe. You are definitely not safe out here!"

"I don't *want* to be safe!" she retorted angrily. "I want to be with you."

Suddenly it all seemed so clear to her, so simple. Why had she let that stupid business with the photographer bother her? She didn't *have* to go to New York. New York was cold and unfriendly and dangerous, everyone knew that. She'd be silly to save and slave and sacrifice just to go to that awful place. People there would probably treat her like a stray dog. She didn't even know how to get on and off a subway. Else Gunderson had been a model in New York City and she hadn't liked it. She'd told Mary Ellen she was much happier in Tarenton, running Marnie's.

Why, she wondered as she turned toward Patrick again, should I let myself in for a rotten time in New York when I can stay right here in Tarenton, where everybody knows me and likes me, and where I can have someone as terrific as Patrick?

Everything was becoming perfectly clear in her mind, as if she was watching a movie. There was New York City, dirty and lonely and dangerous, and then, in the next frame, there were Mary Ellen and Patrick, living in a darling white house in one of the nicest parts of Tarenton because Patrick's business was a huge success. After all, people would always have trash, wouldn't they? And everybody liked Patrick, so how could he possibly not be a success? She'd have all the things she'd always wanted and she wouldn't have to get them all by herself. And best of all, she'd have Patrick!

I probably couldn't make it on my own in New York, anyway, she thought grimly. I probably don't have what it takes to be a model. Reese Oliver would certainly agree with that!

"Patrick," she said, making up her mind, "I'll go in the house, if you'll promise to take me to Walt's party the night before the Garrison game."

"That's a school night," he pointed out. "How come he's not having it after the game?"

"His parents are having a party that Friday night, so Walt's just having a get-together the night before. Okay?"

"I think I can handle that," he said with a grin. He did get tired of just meeting Mary Ellen places and giving her a ride home. This sounded like a real date to him!

"Good." She grinned, too. "Shall we seal it with a kiss?"

97

The kiss he gave her could easily have sealed a peace treaty between two warring nations. Her knees were still shaky when she finally said goodnight and went into the house.

Every time her friends saw her after that, she was with Patrick Henley. Holding his hand in the halls, leaning against a locker, her head tilted up as she talked to him, smiling, and climbing up into the cab of his truck after school or after practice.

At lunch the day before Walt's party, Nancy said, "Well, I see Mary Ellen is eating lunch in some cozy little corner of Tarenton High with one Patrick Henley again. Those two have really found each other, haven't they?"

"Don't get too excited, Nancy," Pres said. "It's probably just a temporary weakness on Mary Ellen's part."

It wasn't that Pres didn't believe Mary Ellen cared for Patrick. He knew she did and he knew that the harmless flirting she sometimes engaged in with Pres was just part of a game they both played very well. But her single-mindedness about leaving Tarenton to do what she wanted had helped him continue his ongoing battle with his father about joining him at Tarenton Fabricators after college. And he wasn't ready to hear that she'd given up on her goals. It might make him question *his*.

To avoid hearing that about Mary Ellen, he quickly changed the subject to Angie's absence at the lunch table.

"She had a dentist appointment," Olivia explained. "But she said she'd be at practice."

Angie didn't really have a dentist appointment. Her teeth were just fine. But her emotions were in a turmoil. A dental appointment had seemed an appropriate excuse for eating her lunch on a bench overlooking the lake, behind the school where no one could see her, since sitting at the same table with a resentful Mary Ellen and a suspicious Nancy would have been about as pleasant as having a tooth drilled. Without novocaine.

And there was still practice. Going to Ardith and saying, I can't come to practice because Mary Ellen's pretending I don't exist these days, would do about as much good as trying to row a boat across the frozen lake. Ardith would never buy such a childish excuse.

If Mary Ellen really cares about Patrick, Angie thought, nibbling on her egg-salad sandwich, the way she seems to right now, why is she still treating me like I'm invisible? If she has what she wants, why should she mind if *I* have what *I* want?

When she saw Mary Ellen in the halls, with or without Patrick at her side, the most Angie got was a cool hi or a nod. Like it's *my* fault Reese wants to take my picture, she thought angrily, staring out across the lake, now beginning to thaw around the edges.

And now she had the party at Walt's to dread. Mary Ellen would be there, and she probably wouldn't even bother to say hello.

I've *got* to talk to her, she vowed, stuffing the remainder of her sandwich into the wrinkled brown paper bag.

The party would be her best chance to get Mary Ellen alone and get this all straightened out. The Garrison game was the following night. If they were going to work together well as a squad, there had to be some kind of peace made between her and Mary Ellen. And if her captain wasn't willing to make the first move, well, she'd have to do it herself.

I'm not giving up this chance to do something fun with my life, she thought as she turned to go back inside. Not even for Mary Ellen. Not even for the squad.

If only Reese would get going on the actual picture-taking. There couldn't possibly be anything about her that he didn't already know, and still he hadn't clicked the shutter once. He'd said he was still looking for a studio. And until he found one and they got this portfolio thing out of the way, she'd be walking on eggs around Mary Ellen, afraid to say a word about it.

Practice was about as much fun as sliding across a bed of nails. Mary Ellen wasn't openly hostile, but she wasn't friendly, either. In the locker room, she talked about Patrick with the same enthusiasm Angie was sure Columbus must have had when he spotted land. But she talked mostly to Olivia and Nancy.

"Mary Ellen," Nancy said once with an amused grin, "you've known Patrick forever. Now all of a sudden you think he's the greatest thing since hot rollers."

"Well, he is!" Mary Ellen said, returning the grin as they left the locker room and headed for the gym. Angie trailed along behind the others.

She was glad for Patrick. Sort of. It was just hard to believe that Mary Ellen was going to stay this enthusiastic about him. And what would happen to Patrick when this cloud nine he was probably on disappeared from underneath him?

Mary Ellen ignored her throughout practice. Several times, Angie got close enough to try to ask if Mary Ellen would talk to her afterwards, but each time she opened her mouth to speak, Mary Ellen suddenly remembered that Nancy's toe touches needed work, or that Walt and Olivia's pony mount stand was just a little bit rusty, or that she was desperately in need of a drink.

Upset by Mary Ellen's efficient coolness, Angie bobbled a simple back arch, landing on the gym floor with her leg underneath her.

"You almost broke your leg!" Mary Ellen called sharply. "Pay attention!"

How can I pay attention, Angie thought resentfully as she got up and dusted off her pink leotard, when you're treating me like dust bunnies under your bed?

"Angie," Ardith called when Angie's foot slid after a cartwheel and landed on Walt's shoe, "what on earth is wrong with you?"

Angie silently told Walt's shoe as she moved

away from it, What's wrong with me is, my captain is pretending I'm a guest from a rival school and Nancy is drilling a hole in my back with her suspicious stares. No one could perform under these circumstances!

By the time practice was finally over, she was beginning to wish she'd never heard of Reese Oliver. Or cheerleading. Or both.

Nancy rode home from practice with Ben, his hair still damp and curly from his shower following basketball practice. She talked about Angie and the photographer all the way home, even though talking about the squad's problems to Josh all the time had been one of the reasons their romance had ended.

When Ben parked the Isuzu in front of her house and turned to get his good-bye kiss, the preoccupied look on her face annoyed him.

"Hey!" he said irritably. "Can we forget about this Reese character? He seemed okay to me. You girls worry too much. Now, c'mere and give me what I've been waiting for all day!"

It would have taken a far greater crisis in Nancy's life than concern over Angie's photographer friend to keep her out of Ben's bearlike embrace. Folded into his barrel chest, her cheek against the rough wool of his plaid jacket, all thoughts of Angie and the squad slid from her mind like chalk marks under an eraser. She lifted her head to give him a kiss.

"That's more like it," Ben murmured, his chin

against the top of her head. "That's my girl."

And she was. His girl. She had accepted the fact that he was a very physical person and in a way, had learned from that. His open affection had freed her a little from her own natural reserve. She knew there were people at school who thought she was a snob. She wasn't. But she was a very private person, not given to touching the way Ben was, and not possessing his natural, outgoing warmth. She knew she wasn't Miss Warmth herself. In a beauty pageant, she might not have done too badly in the looks and figure department, but the Miss Congeniality Award would never be hers.

But she *had* changed, being with Ben. An *ice* sculpture would thaw in his presence. And while his constant need to touch her sometimes made her uncomfortable, especially in public, she knew it was just his way of saying, This is my girl and I'm glad she's with me.

It always amazed her, when she had time to think about it, that she had ended up with one of the sexiest boys in school. Nancy Goldstein, Miss Cool and Careful, with a boy whose grin set hearts pounding all through the halls of Tarenton High.

And her heart was no exception.

"I don't think we got that kiss quite right," Ben said with his famous grin. "Let's try it again. You know what they say. Practice makes perfect, right?"

Right. He'd get no argument from her.

103

CHAPTER

Mary Ellen felt split in two, like one of those chunks of wood Walt was always lugging in from outside to toss into the fireplace. One half of her felt squashed flat, a balloon minus its air. Facing the fact that Angie might soon be on the cover of a national magazine had done that to her. The other half of her felt a sense of relief because of her decision to stay in Tarenton, and excitement about her evening ahead with Patrick.

It was that half that threw caution and thrift aside to buy a new outfit at Marnie's after work that day. Even with her employee's discount, the total amount made her toes curl. She handed Else most of the money she'd withdrawn at noon from her savings account, thinking with a stab of shame that it seemed like enough money to buy food for several drought-stricken countries.

But later, when she'd taken a shower and slipped into the buttery-soft pale blue suede pants and matching jacket, she decided it was worth it. She'd knock Patrick's socks off.

Deciding the outfit called for a sophisticated hairdo, she was carefully curving the wheat-colored strands into a smooth topknot when Gemma burst into the room.

Stopping dead in her tracks, her mouth open in a round "O," she stared before exclaiming, "Mary Ellen! Where did you get that outfit? It's gorgeous!"

"Marnie's," said Mary Ellen casually, as if she wouldn't dream of shopping anywhere else. Gemma sank down on her bed, still staring at her sister.

"Gosh, it must have cost a fortune!" Gemma knew how Mary Ellen struggled to build up her savings account. And she knew *why* she was saving. Mary Ellen had even promised her that she could visit her in New York City one day. She could hardly wait.

Mary Ellen shrugged. "It's only money," she said carelessly, topping off her outfit with tiny gold earrings.

Gemma frowned. Since when was it *only money*? Money had been the second most important thing in Mary Ellen's life, right behind cheerleading, practically forever.

"How come you're all dressed up?"

"Got a date. Walt's having a party and Patrick's picking me up."

"You're dressed like that for a party at Walt's?"

"Gemma," Mary Ellen said patiently, picking up her purse, "a person can't spend her whole life running around in jeans. I *feel* like wearing this, so I'm wearing it."

"Okay. It's just that . . . well, that outfit would be perfect in New York City, but Tarenton?"

Mary Ellen swallowed hard, avoiding Gemma's eyes. "New York's not so hot," she said lightly, in spite of the lump in her throat. "I'm not sure I want to go there, after all. And Tarenton's not so bad, either." Then, tossing a "See you" over her shoulder, she left a very confused Gemma alone.

It took all of Angie's powers of persuasion to talk Reese into going to Walt's party.

"I hate parties," he announced when he showed up at her house and found her all set to leave the house for Walt's. "And since when do your friends throw a party on a school night?"

She explained, adding, "If I don't go, they'll think I'm mad at Mary Ellen. I don't want to make any more trouble than I already have."

The evening would give her the perfect opportunity to fix things with Mary Ellen. And maybe if Nancy got to know Reese a little better, she'd ease up on the suspicion. Although, she had to admit, getting to know Reese was about as easy as climbing Mount Everest wearing ballet slippers.

"Angie," Reese said, leaning against the wall in the foyer, "your friends aren't all that exciting.

106

I always thought cheerleaders were smart. But their idea of an exciting conversation is discussing either a high school basketball game or how to execute the perfect cartwheel."

That wasn't fair. "You haven't spent that much time with them," she protested. "And when you *were* around them, you didn't exactly bend over backwards to be friendly. Give them a chance!"

"Okay, okay!" he said, shrugging to admit defeat. "We'll go. But we're not staying till the wee small hours of the morning, okay? I was all over town today trying to hunt up a studio. I'm beat!"

"We won't be late," she said. "Like you said, it's a school night."

In the car, she asked him if he'd had any luck finding a place. If she could just give Nancy some concrete information about when and where the photo sessions were taking place, maybe the girl would relax.

He shook his head. "That's the trouble with these little one-horse towns," he said with what sounded to her like disgust. "You can never find what you need."

She giggled. "This is not a one-horse town," she said with mock indignation. "Sean Hoffman has his own horse, and so do Suzanne Nicklas and Davey Brunecz. That makes us a three-horse town."

Reese didn't laugh.

"I guess we're going to be stuck with that crummy motel room as our studio," he said. "I'll just have to use more artificial light, that's all."

Angie said nothing. She wasn't keen on the idea of spending even two minutes in a motel room with a guy she hardly knew. But Reese had never made a single move on her. It had been strictly business all the way. So why should she worry now? After all, it wasn't his fault there was no studio for rent in Tarenton. He wasn't any happier about that than she was.

She was a lot more worried about getting back on the track with Mary Ellen and Nancy than she was about Reese making a pass at her.

Sighing, she hoped that this evening at Walt's would iron things out.

It didn't. Instead of meeting Patrick at Walt's and letting him take her home, the way she usually did, Mary Ellen surprised everyone by showing up firmly attached to Patrick. She never once left his side during the entire evening, to everyone's astonishment and Angie's annoyance.

The evening was one of the most irritating nights Angie'd ever spent. Reese refused to hide his boredom, lounging on the couch ignoring everyone and barely bothering to answer Patrick's questions, when all Patrick was trying to do, as anyone with half a brain could see, was be friendly. She was going to tell Reese what she thought of his attitude on the way home, watching as Patrick tried one more time, with the same result. She was annoyed with him, and embarrassed because of him. How could anyone get to know him when he was acting like an ostrich? Any minute now, she expected him to get down and crawl underneath the couch.

And Mary Ellen was pulling that same there-is-no-Angie-Poletti-in-existence-on-this-planet routine again. Angie felt like strangling her. They needed to talk, and Mary Ellen knew it. But every time Angie approached her, Mary Ellen turned to Patrick and said sweetly, "Let's dance," and they were gone, out into the middle of the living room of the log-and-glass house, shaking now with the reverberations of rock and roll at top volume.

"The wildlife around here must be deaf," Angie said crossly as Walt passed her carrying a basket filled with chips.

"That's one of the advantages of living out in the country," he said cheerfully. "No neighbors to complain!"

Angie plunked herself down on the fireplace hearth, watching Mary Ellen and Patrick with sad eyes.

Mary Ellen and Patrick passed her, and she called out, "Mary Ellen! Can I talk to you for a minute?"

Mary Ellen looked over her shoulder as if a puppy had tugged at her pants, and said sweetly, "Oh, gee, Angie, I'm sorry. But Patrick and I are just leaving. I've got a little headache."

And I, Angie thought angrily, have got a major pain in my neck! Its initials are M.E.K.

But she said nothing. What was the use?

Giving up, she returned to Reese, still pouting

on the couch, a paper cup in his hand.

"*They're* leaving," he said resentfully, as Mary Ellen and Patrick waved and went out the door. "Can we get out of here, too?"

"Party-poopers!" Nancy teased. She was sitting on the floor, leaning against Ben. "And that includes Mary Ellen and Patrick, too."

"She's just trying to get away from me," Angie said darkly as she picked up her jacket and purse.

"Can you blame her?" Nancy asked. "Every time she looks at you, she sees the magazine cover you're going to get instead of her."

"That's not my fault!" Angie cried. "And I wouldn't be treating *her* like an allergy if *she* was modeling."

"Oh, come on, Angie," Nancy scolded. "You know perfectly well it doesn't mean as much to you as it does to her!"

"Looks to me," Reese said, tugging on Angie's sleeve, "like Patrick means a lot to her, too. C'mon, Angie, let's go."

"Angie," Nancy continued, ignoring Reese, "didn't you see the way she was dressed tonight? That suede outfit? That's the kind of thing women like my mother wear when they go shopping at the mall or have appointments around town. It doesn't take a shrink to figure out that Mary Ellen is testing the water. She's trying to see how it would feel to stay here in town with Patrick. For good!"

"And not leave at all?" Angie asked, her eyes

registering disbelief. "Mary Ellen? A housewife in Tarenton? She doesn't want that!"

Nancy shrugged. "I didn't say she did. I just said she was testing tonight to see what it would feel like. And I think Patrick knew it. Did you see the way he was looking at her? Like he can't quite believe it, but he *wants* to."

"Poor Patrick," Angie said.

"Poor Reese," Reese complained. "If I don't hit the hay in the next fifteen minutes, my body is going to quit functioning completely. C'mon, now that Dr. Goldstein has analyzed Mary Ellen and Patrick, can we please get out of here?"

Nancy made a face at him and Ben said, "C'mon, Nance, let's us go, too. If we sit here yakking all night, we won't have any time to . . . look at the stars. You know what an astronomy freak I am."

She grinned and got up. "Okay, okay. I'm ready. Angie," Nancy said as Ben helped her with her jacket, "quit worrying, okay? It's putting frown lines on your forehead. You'll age before your time."

Angie thanked Walt for what she called "a great time," although her face clearly said otherwise, and she and Reese left.

On the way home, she tried to tell herself that things would straighten out all by themselves, the way they always did. But then she remembered that all of the worst things that had happened to the squad *hadn't* straightened out all by them-

111

selves. They'd had to work at fixing things. How could they work at it if Mary Ellen wouldn't talk to her?

She also tried to tell herself that if Mary Ellen had decided not to go to New York, it probably *was* because of Patrick. And if that was true, she thought with just a hint of a smile, Patrick probably thinks he's died and gone to heaven.

Patrick didn't feel like he'd died and gone to heaven. This new Mary Ellen, this warm and loving creature sitting beside him with her hand in his as he steered the truck with his other hand, was everything he'd ever wanted — and never expected to have.

But what spoiled it for him was the feeling that she wasn't giving in to her feelings for him. She was just giving *up*. She hadn't come right out and said so, but Patrick was neither blind nor stupid. Every once in a while during the evening when she thought he wasn't looking, her beautiful blue eyes had a lost, faraway look in them.

Patrick wasn't selfish. While being with Mary Ellen made him happier than anything else in his life, it wouldn't work for him if she was secretly miserable.

"I'm *not*, Patrick. Don't be silly!" she insisted when he stopped the truck in front of her house and asked if she was still upset about Reese and Angie. Snuggling against him, she said warmly, "I've never felt as good as I do right now — honest! And that's the truth!"

Was she trying to convince him? Or herself? He just couldn't be sure.

"Look, Mary Ellen," he said, tipping her face up toward his. "I talked to Reese tonight for a few minutes about some of the new lens filters on the market today. He didn't seem to know what I was talking about. I think Nancy's right. I think he's a phony."

Mary Ellen sat up straight, mulling that over. If Reese wasn't really a professional photographer, then his judgment meant zilch and she might still have a chance.

Then she shook her head. "I know you're trying to cheer me up," she said, "but you're wasting your breath. The idea that he's a fake is just too silly. Anyway," she added, putting her arms around his neck, "I don't need cheering up. I feel better about everything than I have in a long time."

"I just don't want to get my hopes up," Patrick said, "and then have you change your mind. We've been on a roller coaster for a long time, Mary Ellen, and after a while it makes me dizzy."

Mary Ellen knew her refusal to make any kind of commitment to Patrick had hurt him. And it had worried her for a long time, aware that at any minute he could find someone who *was* looking for a commitment.

So why didn't she make it now? She was cozy and warm in Patrick's arms, and the way things looked right now, she didn't have any other choices.

But it wasn't as easy to let go of her dream as she'd thought it would be. What if something happened that made her change her mind again? That would be rotten for Patrick! Maybe he wouldn't even be able to forgive her, and then he'd be out of her life forever.

He wasn't demanding anything from her, even now. This whole thing had been *her* idea. All she had to do now was say, "I won't change my mind, Patrick. Ever." And it would all be set.

She couldn't do it. Not yet. She wasn't ready.

"There's only one thing wrong with this evening," she said, looking up at him.

"What?"

"If somebody doesn't kiss me in the next three seconds, I'm going to think I wasted my hard-earned money on this outfit." The truth was, she hated the outfit. It reminded her of the kind of clothes Pres's mother wore when she shopped at Marnie's. It just wasn't *her*.

"Well, I wouldn't want you to think you'd wasted money," Patrick said, nothing in his voice revealing his disappointment. He had hoped she would make some promises, but she hadn't. He shouldn't have expected it. She just wasn't ready. Wishing he hadn't told her he suspected Reese was a phony, annoyed with himself because that suspicion just might have given her new hope, he bent his head and kissed her. If he had to settle for just this right now, so be it. There were worse things than having a beautiful, loving girl in your arms.

114

Like *not* having a beautiful, loving girl in your arms, because you've demanded something she's not ready to give.

Saying her name out loud, he pulled her closer and kissed her again. And at that particular moment, if anyone had asked, they both would have said they had exactly what they wanted.

CHAPTER

12

The next day in study hall, all the excitement of the night before drained out of her, Mary Ellen sat staring out the window, chin in hand. Wearing her cheerleader uniform for the pep rally after school and the home game against Garrison that night, she toyed with the one long, thick braid hanging down her back. She was thinking about Reese Oliver.

Was Patrick right? Were those lens filters something a professional photographer should know about? And wasn't Nancy usually right about people, too? If she didn't trust Reese, maybe it was for a good reason.

If he was a phony — the cornflower blue eyes narrowed — then his judgment didn't mean anything!

Hope crawled into her red-and-white saddle

shoes and made its way up through her body. Had she jumped to the wrong conclusion, thinking Reese's rejection meant she'd never make a good model? Had she given up too quickly? And for the wrong reason?

If I were selling something, she thought, her mind working quickly, which of the cheerleaders would I make my pitch to?

The answer came almost before she'd finished the question: Angie.

It wasn't as if Reese hadn't approached anyone else. He had. But I, she thought, sitting up straight at her desk, was too suspicious, and Nancy wouldn't even give him the time of day. But Angie did. And not because she's stupid or gullible, but because she just trusts people more than Nancy or I do. He must have seen that in her face. That's why he never got back to me, because he knew the minute he saw her that she would at least listen to him without asking a lot of questions.

The question now was, How could anyone be *sure* he's not for real? And if he's not, why is he doing this? For money? Or for something worse? He *did* have a motel room.

Mary Ellen frowned. Why had he approached only cheerleaders? Or had he? She had no way of knowing that he hadn't spoken to other girls in Tarenton. But wouldn't the word have spread? Only Angie and Nancy had mentioned him.

The feeling of relief that spread through her, with the growing certainty that Reese Oliver was a phony, was quickly followed by something else: alarm for Angie.

But she couldn't warn her. It would sound like jealousy. Angie would never buy it, not without proof. And there wasn't any.

But I have to do something, she thought soberly. I have to find some proof. Angie *trusts* him!

The only idea that came to mind was so bizarre she almost discarded it immediately. But when nothing else popped into her head, she decided it might be worth a try. It was, she told herself, better than nothing.

If she hadn't been convinced then that something needed to be done, the pep rally would have made up her mind for her, because Angie performed like a six-year-old taking her first ballet lesson. Her normally smooth movements were as jerky as a fish on a line, and her timing was off. Her face flushed with embarrassment, when a bungled cartwheel brought forth several painfully audible giggles from the spectators. She avoided looking at any of her squadmates as they all ran off the floor after the rally.

"Angie," Ardith called as they were about to enter the locker room, "got a minute?"

Head down, shoulders sagging, Angie walked down the hall and into Ardith's office, closing the door behind her. Five cheerleaders watched her go.

"Good!" Mary Ellen said quickly, grabbing elbows left and right to gather everyone around her. "Now, listen! I'm worried about her and this Oliver person. There's something weird there — Patrick thinks so, and so do I."

"Well, it's about time somebody agreed with me," Nancy said, wiping her forehead with a towel. "So what do we do about it?"

Speaking in a breathless voice, Mary Ellen outlined her plan.

"That's the dumbest thing I've ever heard," Pres said, when she had finished. "What are you, some kind of private eye? You've been watching too much of the boob tube, kiddo."

Walt just looked confused. Olivia linked arms with him. "We'll do anything we can to help Angie," she said.

"I think it's a good idea," Nancy said. "And I'll help."

"Count me out," Pres said. "I'm really not into snooping."

"It's *not* snooping!" Mary Ellen whispered harshly, afraid Ardith's door would open any second and Angie would find them all huddled together in the hall. She would know, of course, who they were discussing. "It's just investigating something for a friend, that's all."

"I think Pres is right," Walt said hesitantly, giving Olivia an embarrassed glance. "It's kind of an invasion of someone's privacy, you know?"

"Walt!" Olivia removed her arm from his.

Mary Ellen sighed. "Okay, guys, that's fine and dandy. We females know everything there is to know about dialing a phone. We'll just do it

119

without you. C'mon, gals, let's get ourselves over to my house. We'll call from there."

As the three of them hurried down the hall, anxious to get out of there before Angie came back, Pres called after them, "You're just jealous, that's all!"

Mary Ellen turned to make a nasty remark, thought better of it, and stuck out her tongue instead.

"Very mature!" he called, laughing.

At the Kirkwood house, Olivia told the others as they gathered around the telephone in the living room, "Angie's going to wonder where we are."

"Well, I just hope Walt and Pres don't tell her," Nancy said, "because she's already uptight and we've got a game tonight."

Mary Ellen found the magazine and leafed through its pages until she found what she was looking for.

"Well, here goes!" she said shakily, joining them on the floor, telephone in hand. It was a long-distance call and she'd have to remember to pay her parents for the charges. But if they learned anything one way or the other, it would be worth it.

To the woman who answered, "American Sports Magazine, may I help you?" Mary Ellen said, "Yes. I'm calling for attorney John Swiss in Boston. Would you by any chance have a current mailing address for the photographer Reese

Oliver? Mr. Swiss has some legal matter to discuss with him."

Olivia put a hand over her mouth to stifle a giggle.

When the woman said, "One moment, please," Mary Ellen covered the mouthpiece and whispered, "I'm an old hand at legal matters. Remember my inheritance? That young lawyer — what was his name? — he taught me everything I — Yes, I'm still here."

A different person was on the line and she had to repeat her request.

"One sec-und, please."

Mary Ellen held her breath, waiting. After several minutes, the second voice came back, saying, "I'm sorry, Madam, but Mr. Oliver is out of the country on assignment."

On the off-chance that someone living in New York City just might consider Tarenton "out of the country," Mary Ellen said, "He's not in the United States?"

"No, ma'am. Mr. Oliver is currently on assignment in the Sudan."

The Sudan? Mary Ellen thanked the woman, and hung up, a grim smile on her face. Geography had never been her strongest subject, but she knew the Sudan wasn't anywhere near Tarenton.

"He's not even in the country," she announced smugly, looking at Nancy and Olivia.

They sat there silently for a few minutes.

"Poor Angie," Olivia said softly. "She's going to feel like such a fool."

"Do you realize what this means?" Mary Ellen said gleefully. "This means the guy has no credentials to judge who's photogenic and who's not. I can't believe I let his opinion throw me for a loop like that!"

"Mary Ellen," Nancy said, "quit thinking about yourself and concentrate on how we're going to get Angie out of this."

"We'll just tell her the truth, that's all," Mary Ellen answered, putting the telephone back on the coffee table.

"I don't think she'll believe us," Olivia said. "She'll just think you guys are jealous. She already thinks it. That's why she's been goofing up so much on the squad. She thinks you hate her, Mary Ellen."

"That's ridiculous," Mary Ellen said, secure in her knowledge now that Reese was a phony. "Why would I be jealous of a fake?"

Then, after a minute, she added, "But I think you're right. I don't think she'll believe us. He could always tell her they have orders at the magazine not to give out his address."

"We need more proof," Nancy said flatly. "And we need it fast!"

Mary Ellen nodded. "But right now," she said, getting up and brushing off her red wool shirt, "we've got a game. That comes first. Maybe tomorrow we can get together and plan some strategy. We'll figure out something."

On the way back to school, Olivia mentioned Angie's pathetic performance at the pep rally.

"It's your fault, Mary Ellen," she said matter-of-factly. "Angie thinks you hate her and she can't relax. Maybe you'd better say something to her before the game, or she's going to foul everybody up."

"I think she's just uptight about this picture-taking business," Mary Ellen defended herself. "I just hope Ardith said all the right words to her this afternoon."

"So do I," Nancy agreed. "Because if we look lousy tonight, Ben will be in a foul mood. He hates it when anything about Tarenton looks less than wonderful in front of his old school."

"Coach probably got through to Angie," Mary Ellen said optimistically. "I know she always got through to *me* when we had our cozy little chats."

But Ardith was having a hard time talking with Angie.

It always upset her when any member of the squad was in bad form, but when that member happened to be Angie, she was surprised as well as dismayed. Angie was the most easygoing of the girls, and Ardith sometimes forgot that she had the same emotional problems as most girls her age.

She had a feeling that just saying, Shape up, Angie, wasn't going to do it this time.

"So," she said to the dejected cheerleader sitting slumped in the vinyl chair opposite the coach's desk, "what's up?"

Angie shook her head. "I'm sorry," she said.

"I know I was terrible out there. I just seem to be going from bad to worse." She looked at Ardith with sad, dark eyes. Her hair hung down her back, curling up slightly on the ends, the sides feathered away from her face.

She looks very tired, Ardith thought with surprise. I don't remember ever seeing her look so wiped-out before.

"Can I help?" While she was concerned about the squad's performance that evening, she was also very fond of Angie Poletti and hated seeing the girl unhappy.

Angie hesitated for a minute before blurting out, "I feel like I'm all alone out there," she said in a low voice. "And I don't like it. It makes me nervous. But Mary Ellen treats me like a stranger and Nancy keeps looking at me funny."

"Funny?"

"Like she doesn't trust me. Then I do something stupid out on the floor and I think she's right not to trust me. And then I do something stupid *again*."

"Want to tell me what's going on?" Ardith asked casually. She made it a strict policy never to pry into her squad's personal problems. But if Angie chose to unload on her, well, listening was part of a coach's job, too.

Angie was tempted. Without the squad behind her, Ardith was the only one left for her to talk to.

But she shook her head. "Can't," she said huskily. "But thanks, anyway. I'll handle it, I guess. It's just that . . . well, when people treat you like you're weird, you start to act that way. Don't you think so?"

Ardith nodded. "Yes, I do think so," she said firmly. "I see that all the time. But you," she added, "mustn't let that happen to you. Do you respect my opinion, Angie?"

"Sure. Of course I do," Angie answered, standing up.

"Then listen to me when I say you're not weird and you most definitely are not stupid."

Angie flushed a deep red. "I wasn't fishing for compliments, Mrs. Engborg — honest!"

"I know you weren't. I'm just giving you my opinion."

Angie wanted to believe her. She wanted to believe that *someone* was on her side. So that she wouldn't feel so alone.

"Now," the coach said, leading Angie to the door, "we have a very important game tonight. As always, I expect you to stick your personal problems into your gym bag and hide it in your locker for the duration. Understood?"

Angie nodded. "I'll be fine," she said as she opened the door. "I promise. And thanks for talking to me."

"Just do your best," Ardith said, and closed the door after Angie.

CHAPTER

13

Mary Ellen, convinced now that Reese wasn't really a professional photographer and therefore couldn't be expected to know a terrific model if one walked up and bit him, was generous in her relief. In the locker room before the game, she made every effort to show Angie that all was forgiven. She welcomed her with a big smile, called out to her as they made last-minute adjustments on their hair, and even gave her a casual pat on the shoulder as they ran out of the locker room and into the gym.

But Angie wasn't buying it. She had no idea why Mary Ellen had suddenly changed her attitude, but her captain's earlier coolness still stung.

She never bothered to apologize, she thought resentfully, as they all gathered around Mary

Ellen to check out the evening's roster. She hasn't wished me good luck with my portfolio and she hasn't asked me if we've taken any pictures yet. So whatever the reason is for her good mood, as far as I'm concerned it doesn't have anything to do with me. It's probably because of Patrick.

But if it was Patrick, then why, when Mary Ellen glanced over at her as they took their positions on the floor for the "Welcome" cheer, were Mary Ellen's eyes filled with concern? Concern that seemed to be directed at Angie.

Why, she wondered as they built a human pyramid, is Mary Ellen looking at me as though she's worried about me?

Maybe she's just afraid I'm going to make a horrible mess of things tonight like I did this afternoon, she thought, climbing up to take her place on Walt's shoulders. That's probably it. Well, I'll just have to show her, that's all.

Buoyed by her talk with Ardith and determined to show Mary Ellen that she could be trusted to do her job, Angie performed flawlessly throughout the game. Her face was strained with nervous tension, but her body behaved beautifully.

They hadn't had too many games that were as close as this one.

Nancy watched with shining eyes as Ben whizzed down the court, the basketball dancing under his touch, slam-dunking it into the net time and time again. When he raised the score to 18 over Garrison's 16, she gladly cooperated

127

with Mary Ellen's suggestion for a series of back flips to salute him.

At halftime the score was tied, 28-28. Their halftime performance was as smooth as silk, all of them tightly wound with excitement and enthusiasm, giving a healthy bounce to their gymnastic routines.

The change in Mary Ellen hadn't escaped Patrick's eyes. In the stands, looking down upon the swirl of red-and-white out on the floor, he thought, Something's happened. She's her old self again. Her old bounce and enthusiasm were back, and even from high up in the stands, he was sure her blue eyes were sparkling.

That's not because of me, he thought heavily. I know it's not. Then what? What was it that had put new life into that beautiful body?

He'd have to wait until later to find out. But he had a feeling he wasn't going to like the answer. If she was feeling better, he was glad for her. He *was*. It was himself he was worried about.

Mary Ellen didn't look as if she needed to cling to him tonight.

The second half of the game flew by in a blur of pounding feet thundering up and down the court, whistles shrilling through the air, and shouts and screams of joy and disappointment.

"Take it away!
Take it away!"

. . . the Varsity Cheerleaders screamed, mega-

128

phones in hand, as the Garrison center raced up the court, dribbling furiously.

> "Two points!
> Two points!
> Two more points!"

. . . they shouted frantically with the score 36-36 and Donny Parrish making his way through some strong defense to the Garrison basket.

The ball arced in the air and then went smoothly through the net, and the cheerleaders shouted:

> "Yay, Team!
> Yay, TEAM!
> Yay, Wolves!"

During a time-out, Mary Ellen ran out onto the floor, followed by her squad. Lining up in front of the bleachers, they shouted:

> "We're the red.
> We're the white,
> We're gonna take this game tonight!
> We're the white,
> We're the red,
> We're gonna win, that's what we said!"

Her cheeks red with excitement and exertion, her blue eyes flashing, and her wheat-colored braid swinging over her shoulder, Mary Ellen put her megaphone to her mouth and shouted with the others, "What did we say?"

The audience shouted back, "We're gonna win!"

Again, "What did we say?"

And the audience came back with, "We're gonna win!"

By the time Tarenton captured the ball in the last seconds of the game, the crowd was on its feet, and frantically shouted commands from both sets of spectators filled every square inch of the gym.

With the score 52-52 and time running out, Ben stopped in midcourt to lift his arms high in the air and propel the ball toward the basket to a chorus of nervous "Oohs." He had never shot from that distance before. The ball went up, up, back down and . . . into the net.

The crowd went wild and Ben's teammates raced to congratulate him, slapping him on the back and pumping his hands. The cheerleaders ran out onto the floor, jumping, shouting, laughing, as the court filled with people.

"Wasn't Ben fantastic!" Nancy cried as they made their way through the crowd to the locker room. "Wait'll I get my hands on him! He'll be so glad he made that last basket!"

Hurrying through her shower and makeup routine, she dressed quickly in gray slacks and a peach mohair sweater. There was no postgame party scheduled, so there was no point in staying in her uniform. She was glad there was no party; all she wanted now was to be alone with Ben.

But when she got outside, entering a hall still crowded with shouting, laughing students, Ben wasn't alone. With him was a man Nancy recognized as the chubby, balding Garrison basketball coach.

"I just wanted Coach to meet you," Ben said, making the introductions. He grinned proudly. "I wanted him to see for himself how well I'm doing over here."

They were making polite small talk when the coach looked away for a second and called out, "Hey, Billy, how's it goin'?"

When Nancy casually looked up, her eyes widened as she saw the person the coach had called "Billy."

It was Reese Oliver.

As she stared, Reese stumbled, his face flushing scarlet, ducked his head, and hurried away.

"Excuse me, Coach," she said quickly, "but that guy you just called Billy. . . . Who is he?"

"Him? Oh, that's Billy Slocum."

"Billy Slocum?" Her eyes met Ben's, as if to say, See? I told you Reese was a phony! He said nothing, but she could tell he was waiting for the coach's information on Billy Slocum.

"Yeah, Garrison boy, born and raised. Graduated three, maybe four years ago." The coach shook his head. "Tried out for basketball every year. Never did make it. 'Course, he was a good fifty pounds overweight in those days." He thought for a minute before adding, "Had real bad skin problems, too. Glad to see it's cleared up. Poor Billy never did fit in anywhere. So he was a real loner."

Knowing how important it was to be certain, Nancy asked, "But Coach, if he graduated that long ago and he's changed so much, how can you be so sure that that boy you just saw was Bill Slocum?"

The coach looked at her as if she'd just asked him how much two plus two was. "Why, honey," he said easily, "I see Billy from time to time. He never did leave town. Lives with his aunt in that big brick house on Walnut Street, just the two of them. Billy works at the camera shop on Main Street. Doesn't have much to do with anyone, though."

Camera shop. Nancy grinned at Ben.

The coach took a toothpick from his jacket pocket and began chewing on it, while Nancy and Ben tried to digest the information he had just given them.

"Glad to see Billy's still following basketball," the coach added. "Never did miss a single game when he was a student."

Then he looked at Nancy and asked, "Know Billy, do you?"

Nancy hesitated for just a second before answering, "No. I thought I did. But I guess I was wrong."

132

When the coach had gone, Nancy looked at Ben silently.

"Okay, okay!" he said, taking her hand and leading her toward the exit. "So you were right, gorgeous. Feel better now?"

"No," she said, "that's just it." He pushed the door open and they walked to the Isuzu. "I feel rotten. I should tell Angie right away, but I don't think I want to do it alone. I'd better talk to Mary Ellen first. And Livvy. Maybe together we can all figure out the best way to tell her that she's being taken for a ride by that guy."

"What's he after?" Ben asked, as they pulled out of the parking lot. "Or shouldn't I ask?"

"I don't know. Angie insists he hasn't made a pass at her. Maybe he just wants money. But he was *in* the Poletti house, so he must know they're not exactly rich. It doesn't make sense."

They rode in silence for a while. Then Ben put a hand on her knee and said, "You're not gonna worry about this all night, are you? I mean, I figured after the game I played tonight, you'd want to give me a gold medal."

"Right!" she agreed, moving closer and squeezing his hand. He *had* been great tonight, and this was one relationship she didn't want to grind into the ground with her worries about the squad. She wasn't going to spoil tonight by worrying about something she couldn't do anything about until tomorrow.

"You were wonderful tonight!" she said enthusiastically, smiling over at him.

133

"Are you all talk and no action?" he asked, returning the smile.

"No, I'm not," she said, leaning against his shoulder.

Only a tiny part of her brain refused to stop worrying about Angie and Reese.

Reese had hurried outside when the Garrison coach greeted him, but not before he'd seen Nancy and Ben standing with the man. He should have been more careful. Anyone with more brains than a tin can would know enough to watch out for the Garrison coach at a Garrison game!

He'd had to wait outside, behind a parked van, until he saw the coach leaving with his team. Then he went back inside to get Angie.

"I think we should take pictures tomorrow," he said, when they were on their way home in his little car. "I guess I know enough about you now. Gotta be in the motel, though. There just isn't any place else. Sorry."

"That's okay," Angie said matter-of-factly. She wasn't the least bit worried about Reese giving her any trouble. She was sure she could trust him that way. What she'd really been worried about was that he was never going to get going on the actual picture-taking. And now, finally, here it was!

Maybe it would help her feel better. Although Mary Ellen had been more relaxed around her tonight and the squad had performed well, she really hadn't been comfortable. She still felt very much alone.

"What should I wear?" she asked him, beginning to feel excited. The pictures would be taken and developed, Reese would show them to the magazine people, and maybe . . . just maybe . . . she could have a wonderful new future. Christie Brinkley, watch out! she thought, grinning.

"Your uniform," he answered, "what else?"

She glanced over at him, surprised. He seemed edgy tonight. Professional jitters, maybe? Well, *she* was a little nervous, why shouldn't he be?

"The uniform will help sell the pictures," he explained. "*Everybody* loves cheerleaders. Especially the cheerleaders themselves."

"Reese! That's not very nice!" Then, more quietly, she asked, "Do you really think we're conceited?"

He shook his head. "Forget it. Listen, I'm going to need the rest of the money tomorrow morning. I've got to buy some lights."

Angie frowned. "You mean I have to pay before I even see the pictures?"

"You don't *have* to do *anything*!" he said sharply. "But if you want the best pictures possible, you need the best lighting possible. That means I've got to buy additional equipment. And that means money. Got it?"

She nodded.

"But if you don't trust me with the money, we can just forget the whole thing."

"Don't be silly. Of course I trust you. The drive-in window at the bank is open tomorrow morning. I'll get the money then."

"Then meet me at the motel at one o'clock and we'll get this show on the road. You won't be sorry, Angie."

CHAPTER

14

Mary Ellen wouldn't have told Patrick about her telephone call to *American Sports* magazine if he hadn't pressed her. But it was difficult to hide her feelings, and Patrick knew her moods as well as he knew his own name. Something was making her feel better, and he wanted to know what it was.

Even as Patrick asked, the optimism that came as naturally to him as tying his shoes let him hope that she would say, Nothing, Patrick. I'm just really glad to be with you tonight, that's all. But the realism that came just as naturally to him knew she wouldn't say that.

She didn't say that. Turning sideways on the seat to face him, she told him what they'd found out, eagerness and excitement in every word.

He pulled the truck into her driveway and turned off the ignition.

"So," he said, staring out the windshield, "this guy supposedly taking Angie's pictures, instead of yours, is a phony."

"Yes," Mary Ellen said, nodding and wondering why Patrick wasn't looking at her. She moved closer and peered up into his face. "You were right about him. Think you're smart, don't you?" she added playfully.

He didn't smile. But he did look at her. "I'm smart enough to know your good mood doesn't have anything to do with me," he said in a grim voice. "So how about if we just cut this evening short, okay? It's late."

Mary Ellen stared at him, realizing that she shouldn't have told him about Reese. Not yet. Why was she always forgetting how smart Patrick really was? He knew perfectly well what this discovery about Reese meant to their relationship. She should have found a gentler way to tell him.

"Patrick, I — "

"Hey, it's okay!" She could see his jaw outlined through the darkness. When it was set like that, like something on Mount Rushmore, nothing she could say or do would soften his mood. Trying to would be about as useful as attacking a brick wall with a feather.

"C'mon, I'll walk you in," he said brusquely, yanking the truck door open.

He didn't even kiss her good-night. He just said,

"See you," and turned and hurried down the path to the truck.

Mary Ellen watched him go. So she'd got something back today that she'd thought she'd lost: her future as a model in New York City. Did that mean losing Patrick?

She didn't see why. Couldn't they just have what they'd had before Reese came along? What was the matter with Patrick, anyway? It wasn't as though she'd promised him anything. Not really. Not in so many words, anyway.

He should be glad for her . . . if he really cared about her.

Well, Patrick would just have to take a backseat right now, because the situation involving Angie and Reese was much more crucial. She'd put Patrick first once before, and it had nearly ruined her relationship with Angie. She wasn't about to make the same mistake twice.

She'd call Nancy and Olivia first thing in the morning. There was no point in calling Pres or Ben or Walt because they all thought she was just jealous, and wouldn't believe her claim that Reese was a fake.

We don't need the guys, she decided as she turned and went into the house. The three of us can handle it alone. We'll come up with something.

Torn by relief at finding Reese's judgment unimportant and sadness over Patrick's hurt feelings, and nagged by worry over Angie, she tossed and turned most of the night.

Saturday morning, she awoke feeling as old and rusted as her creaking bedsprings. Still in her robe, she was heading for the telephone when it rang in the hall outside her room.

It was Nancy, and her first few sentences to Mary Ellen were so rushed it was hard to make sense of what she was saying.

"Nancy, slow down," Mary Ellen said impatiently. "Who's Billy Slocum?"

"Reese," Nancy said just as impatiently. "Reese Oliver is Billy Slocum. He's from Garrison, lived there all his life. He's no more a professional photographer than I am!"

"Garrison? He's from Garrison?"

Nancy explained about talking to the basketball coach. "We've got to find Angie and tell her."

"Wait a minute," Mary Ellen warned. "Just wait a minute. You don't expect Angie to believe a story like that, do you? She's not going to believe anything *we* tell her about Reese. She's so sure we're jealous, she'll think we're making it up."

"Well, what do you suggest then?" Nancy asked sarcastically. "I mean, we can't just let her go ahead with whatever this guy has in mind for her."

"I have an idea," Mary Ellen said, thinking quickly. "Can you get your father's car?"

"Sure. Why?"

"We'll take a run over to Garrison and check out the public library for old copies of the yearbook. If we can find a picture of Reese Oliver as Billy Slocum, we can take it to Angie. A picture is proof positive, right?"

"That's a great idea!"

Mary Ellen flushed with pleasure. It wasn't every day that Nancy Goldstein paid her a compliment.

"I'll call Olivia," Nancy offered. "Pick you up in half an hour?"

"Make it forty-five minutes. I'll be ready."

Slipping into jeans and a crisp white shirt under a blue V-necked sweater, Mary Ellen wondered what the fake photographer wanted from Angie. Was it something as simple as why they'd all been warned for years not to talk to strangers? Or was it money? Or was it something else?

Pulling on brown suede boots, she decided there wasn't any point in trying to figure out someone like this guy, who operated in the Twilight Zone. She had no experience that would give her a clue about his motives.

They talked about him all the way to Garrison, a forty-minute drive.

"I wish I knew what he wants from her," Nancy said, echoing Mary Ellen's earlier thoughts. The day was misty and cool, with a faint drizzle spotting the windshield. The wipers drummed back and forth with an annoying, dragging sound.

"Me, too," Mary Ellen agreed. "Maybe it's just money. But then you'd think he'd have picked someone with more of it — like Vanessa."

141

Olivia, still half asleep, nodded drowsily. "I don't want to think about it," she murmured, leaning against Mary Ellen as Nancy negotiated a curve. "Anyway, it doesn't matter what he wants, because we're going to stop him, right?"

"Right!" her companions agreed, with more enthusiasm than they actually felt.

"I wish I could have told Walt," Olivia said. "I always feel safer when he's around."

She might just as well have come right out and announced that the male sex was superior to its counterpart. They both jumped on her at the same time.

"Olivia Evans! You traitor!"

"Livvy! Shame on you. You don't think we women can handle this?"

Immediately ashamed, Olivia flushed and shook her head. "I'm sorry, I'm sorry! I didn't mean it! Of course we can handle it."

"Anyway," Mary Ellen commented as they drove along Main Street in Garrison, searching for the library, "it's not our fault the guys all think we're just jealous of Angie and that our imaginations are working overtime."

"Right," Nancy agreed. "There's the library. I'll park across the street." She went up to the corner and turned around and, as they pulled up in front of the big gray building, added, "All I hope is, we're not on a wild-goose chase here. I don't think I could deal with that."

She didn't have to. They found what they were looking for in the second yearbook they opened.

Although the name under the picture read: SLOCUM, WILLIAM E., and although the face was much rounder, there was no mistaking the bushy eyebrows and rabbity eyes.

The face in the picture definitely belonged to the person they all knew as Reese Oliver.

"He must not have been any big deal on campus," Mary Ellen pointed out. "There's only one activity listed under his name. And look which one it is."

It was Photography Club.

They all sat at the long table in a back room of the library, staring at each other.

"So now what do we do?" Nancy asked bluntly. "We don't have a card for this library."

"Doesn't matter," Mary Ellen said. "There's an intercounty lending program here. I have my Tarenton card with me. We can use that."

A few minutes later, the yearbook tucked safely under Olivia's arm, they hurried to the car and began the drive back to Tarenton.

Pleased with themselves, they chattered excitedly about their find, until Nancy sobered all of them by saying, "Angie isn't going to take this news very well."

"No," Olivia said slowly, looking down at the book in her hands, "she's not. I think she was really excited about this whole modeling thing."

I certainly would have been, Mary Ellen thought grimly, aware for the first time that it could easily have been *her* they were hurrying to protect.

Aloud, she said, "It's funny. I didn't trust the guy at first, and then I was mad at myself for *not* trusting him, and now I find out I was right in the first place. That should make me feel good, but it doesn't."

"I just feel sorry for Angie," Olivia said. "She was feeling so bad when Arne split with her, and then she felt better because Reese said she could be a model. I know she was worried about *you*, Mary Ellen, because you were mad at her, but I still think she was excited about the pictures."

"I wasn't mad at her," Mary Ellen defended herself. "I was just . . . disappointed, that's all."

"Well, you weren't very nice to her," Nancy accused, "and the only reason you treated her like a human being last night was that you already suspected Reese was a fraud."

Mary Ellen shrugged. "I'll make it up to her."

"Well, we have no choice," Olivia pointed out. "We can't just let her go on thinking this guy is for real."

They all agreed that would be stupid, even cruel.

"I just hope she doesn't hate us for telling her," Olivia added. "She's been tense enough lately, and this whole business might really knock her out of her socks."

It had stopped raining and the sun was just beginning to shine down on Tarenton as they entered the city limits. They drove straight to Angie's house. None of them were looking forward to the task at hand, and all they wanted was to get the job done.

Andrew answered the door.

"Great game last night," Mary Ellen praised. "Is Angie here?"

Andrew grinned in response to the compliment. "Thanks. Nope, she's not here. Sorry."

"Do you know where she is?" Olivia asked, keeping the yearbook hidden in the folds of her yellow raincape.

"Yeah. I think Reese is taking some pictures of her today. About time, if you ask me."

By concentrating very hard, they all managed to refrain from exchanging glances. Instead, they kept their eyes on Angie's tall, dark-haired, younger brother. No one wanted to make him suspicious.

"Do you know where they might be?" Nancy asked him.

"Yep. He couldn't find a studio here," Andrew said in a matter-of-fact voice, "so he's taking the pictures at his motel." He shrugged. "I guess Angie trusts Reese. I tried to stop her, but you know Angie. I think she's nuts going to his motel room."

"Mary Ellen," Nancy said as she started the car, "I hope you know where Reese is staying, because we forgot to ask Andrew."

"Nancy, this is not exactly New York City. It's not as if tourists are falling all over themselves trying to get to Tarenton. There's only one decent motel in town and that's where he's staying."

She gave Nancy directions, and they all sat back and tried to relax, but found it impossible. They were all imagining the look in Angie's eyes when she found out she'd been duped.

"Sometimes I wish I was only four years old again," Mary Ellen said into the silence. She was thinking of Patrick's hurt as well as Angie's. "Everything was so much easier then."

Nancy nodded. Olivia, remembering the hospitals and the doctors in her life when she was young, said nothing. But at least, she thought, no one was hurting me deliberately, the way Reese is hurting Angie.

"All I want to know," she announced as they drove up a curving driveway to a sign reading: OFFICE, "is why he's doing this."

"Well, whatever his reason is," Mary Ellen said, getting out of the car, "it had better be good!"

The three of them went inside to find out which room was registered to a Mr. Reese Oliver.

Or a Mr. William E. Slocum.

CHAPTER

Angie, wearing her cheerleading uniform, her hair shining, sat on a straight-backed wooden chair in a corner of the motel room, watching Reese tack up a white sheet on the wall to use as a backdrop.

She had handed him an envelope filled with a good portion of her savings earlier that morning. And ever since then, her stomach had been in knots. Her mother had said the decision to spend the money should be her own, and she'd *made* that decision. But she was beginning to feel uncomfortable about it. So much money . . . it had taken her a long time to save it. Was it going to be worth it?

Watching Reese maneuver a metal light stand into position at an angle to the backdrop, she was impressed with his professionalism. He certainly seemed to know what he was doing.

What if he didn't? Doubt filled her like air forced into a balloon. She didn't want it, and she fought against it, but it was no use. The doubt remained.

She wasn't sure why. Maybe it was the exchange of money before any pictures had actually been taken. When she took film to Fotomat she didn't pay for it until the pictures were processed. What was to stop him from taking the money and leaving?

You sound like Nancy, she scolded herself mentally. And maybe that was part of it, too — that Nancy didn't trust Reese and made no bones about it. Not that Nancy Goldstein knew everything there was to know in the world. Still. . . .

"Give me a hand here, will you?" Reese called, as he wrestled with a large white umbrella, trying to attach it to the light pole.

She got up stiffly and went to help him. I'm being silly, she thought. Mary Ellen was going to take Reese up on his offer to photograph her, and she's no dummy. If he hadn't decided on me, she'd be here right this minute.

That made her feel better. "Okay!" she said, with the umbrella attached and the lights plugged in. "Where do you want me?"

Before he could answer, there was a loud knock on the door, followed immediately by a series of knocks. Angie's eyes widened as she heard her name called.

"Angie!" That was Mary Ellen's voice. What

was she doing here? "Angie, let us in!" As Reese and Angie stood in the middle of the room, confused, Nancy's and Olivia's voices joined Mary Ellen's, calling Angie's name.

"What's going on?" Reese asked sharply, his pale cheeks reddening, matching the wool shirt he was wearing with baggy tan pants. "What are *they* doing here?"

"*I* don't know," Angie answered. "Maybe the coach called a meeting or something."

"Well, ignore them," he said, picking up his camera. "Maybe they'll go away. You're busy here. You don't have time for any stupid meeting."

But they didn't go away.

"Angie, if you don't let us in right now, we're going to get a key from the manager."

What on earth were they making such a fuss about? Embarrassed and puzzled, Angie looked at Reese.

"I've got to let them in," she explained, "or they won't have to *go* to the manager — he'll be up here to find out what all the racket's about."

"Oh, for Pete's sake!" he said in disgust, and flopped down on the gold-and-orange-flowered bedspread.

Angie pulled the door open.

The three of them stood in front of her in jeans and raincoats, hair damp and curling, cheeks red. Olivia was clutching a large book.

"What are you *doing* here?" Angie asked. "What's wrong?"

"Are you okay?" Mary Ellen asked her, pushing past the open door. Nancy and Olivia followed.

With all three of them standing in the room, there didn't seem to be any point to keeping the door open, so she closed it, frowning.

"Of course I'm okay. Why wouldn't I be?"

She saw the look that passed from one to the other and got an "oh-oh" feeling in her stomach. Something wasn't right, and the looks on their faces told her that the something that wasn't right was in *her* life, not theirs.

"What is it?" she demanded.

Mary Ellen took a deep breath and let it out. "Maybe you should ask Mr. Slocum," she said, watching Reese carefully.

He shook his head and made a face of disgust and a sound like warm soda fizzing in a glass.

"Who's Mr. Slocum?" Angie asked, frowning. She was standing against the white backdrop and Mary Ellen, looking at her, thought with surprise, She looks good standing there. That *would* make a great magazine cover!

Then she remembered that there wasn't going to be any magazine cover. And she was deeply ashamed of the relief she'd felt when she found out Reese wasn't Reese.

But he didn't look ashamed. He just looked annoyed, and his face wore that pouty look again, the one she'd noticed when she first met him.

"Who's Mr. Slocum?" Angie repeated when no one answered her.

They didn't want to tell her. Now that they were all here, and could see Angie standing in her uniform among all the camera equipment, waiting to pose, everything seemed different. They were all thinking the same thing: Would it really hurt to let her pose? She'd find out eventually, they knew, that it hadn't been the real thing. But did they have to shoot her down right this minute?

It was Mary Ellen who decided. She knew, better than Nancy or Olivia, what pinching pennies really meant, and she knew that Angie had to do a lot of it. It wasn't fair of Reese to take her money for a lie.

"Show her the picture," Mary Ellen told Olivia, still holding the yearbook.

"That a Garrison yearbook you've got there?" Reese asked casually, as if it was no big deal, as if the picture inside it wasn't going to show him up for the fake he was. Mary Ellen stared at him. He certainly was playing it cool.

Olivia, ignoring him, found the right page and held the book out to Angie. Tapping a finger on the picture, she said, "That's Mr. Slocum. Billy Slocum."

Angie looked at it. Then she looked up at Olivia. "Well? Who is he?"

"Don't you recognize him?"

"I don't know that guy. I don't know anybody in Garrison, you know that."

"Yes. You do." Olivia said softly. "Look at the picture again."

Mary Ellen hated the expression on Reese's

face. He was lounging back on the bed watching Angie, with contempt written all over his face. His upper lip was curved into a sneer.

He can't wait for her to find out, she thought, astonished. He *wants* her to know. But why?

The three girls watched Angie's face, and sadness for her, mixed with a certain amount of guilt for being responsible for what she was feeling overcame them, as the truth slowly dawned on Angie.

Staring at the picture, she frowned, peered at it more closely, and then very slowly lifted her dark eyes from the page and moved them toward Reese.

If she had any doubts about the girls being right about the identity of the yearbook subject, they'd disappeared when she saw the expression on his face.

"I . . . I don't understand," she said to him. "This is *you* in here? You're this Slocum, William? Your name isn't Reese Oliver?"

"Billy," he said lazily. "Nobody calls me William. Except my aunt, and she doesn't count."

"Billy? Billy Slocum? That's your name?" She sagged against the sheet-covered wall. "Then . . . then you're not really a photographer?"

He shrugged. "I take pictures," he said. "Who doesn't? But I'm better than most."

Angie waited a minute or two before saying through lips numb with shock, "But you're *not* Reese Oliver, the one whose name was in the magazine?"

Another shrug. Mary Ellen had to clench her fists to keep from running over to the bed and slapping his face.

"I didn't think the guy would mind if I borrowed his name for a while."

There was, then, a long silence. The girls kept their eyes on Angie's face, drained now of all color. As the whole truth sank in, her beautiful dark eyes filled with tears.

"Oh, no," she whispered finally. "No. I'm not that stupid. I'm not."

"Guess again," Billy Slocum said flatly.

"Oh, shut up!" Mary Ellen shouted. "You creep! Just shut up!"

Olivia's heart ached for Angie. She knew how she felt. She had, on at least one horrible occasion that she remembered very clearly, become closely acquainted with feeling foolish and stupid. She'd hated it.

"If you're stupid," Mary Ellen said clearly, aiming her words toward Angie, "that makes two of us. Because I would have done it, too, if El Creepo here hadn't decided on you."

Angie looked at her, doubt written all over her face. "Oh, sure."

"I mean it. And you know what else? He was right. If a photographer was looking for a healthy, all-American, athletic type, you'd be perfect. You look great in front of that backdrop."

"You do, Angie," Olivia echoed. "It's not your fault this guy isn't the real thing. You'd make a great magazine cover."

"Oh, *stop* it!" Angie cried, tears sliding down her cheeks. "You don't have to treat me like a stupid child just because I acted like one. Stop patronizing me!"

That shocked them into silence.

Swiping at her tears with the back of her hand, Angie turned toward Billy. "Why?" she demanded. "Why did you do this? I've never done anything to you. I don't even know you!"

He stopped slouching and sat up straight. His eyes narrowed. "Well, I know you!" he said coldly. He looked at the other three girls, watching him. "I know all of you. You're all alike, in your cute little skirts, your sweaters with the big red letter on the front. Dancing around in front of everyone out there on the gym floor, as if you were princesses giving your subjects a big thrill."

The bitterness in his voice stunned all of them. They stood perfectly still, Angie still against the wall, the other girls grouped together in the center of the room, all of them facing Billy, staring at him.

"You walk through the halls with your noses up in the air, too good for us commoners," he continued, his words hammering away at them. "The only guys you lend your precious presence to are the jocks, the Student Council guys, or class officers."

"That's not true!" Mary Ellen cried angrily, forgetting for the moment that Patrick was a member of the Student Council and Ben was definitely a jock.

154

"Oh, yes, it is," he said, sneering at her. "The rest of us are invisible to cheerleaders. You don't even see us. We don't exist for you."

No one knew what to say, how to stop his hateful words.

"You saw what I looked like in high school, in that yearbook," he went on relentlessly. "Look me in the face and tell me honestly that any of you would have even known my name. Or *cared* what it was."

He paused, and Mary Ellen jumped in, her tone of voice defensive. "Well, I, for one, wouldn't have cared," she said heatedly, "but not because of your looks. You're just not a very nice person!"

He made a sound of disgust and shook his head. "Well, maybe I was — once," he said, tipping his head to one side and fixing his pale eyes on her. "Maybe when I started high school, I was just like everybody else . . . or thought I was."

"What changed you?" Angie asked quietly.

He laughed, a harsh and bitter sound. "Too many girls like you," he answered. "The pretty ones, the popular ones, the ones who looked right through me. Most of them wore outfits just like you're wearing right now."

"That's why you made those sarcastic remarks about cheerleaders," Angie said, her eyes wide. "You hate us!"

"Maybe you just never gave those girls a chance," Nancy said.

"Oh, I gave them a chance, all right," he said bitterly. "One girl laughed right in my face. And after I'd turned around and walked away, I heard her telling a friend that I'd just asked her out. The way she put it was, 'Can you believe that jerk actually thought I might be seen in public with him?' Her birdbrain friend got a real charge out of that."

"They were featherheads," Mary Ellen said flatly.

Ignoring that, he continued. "Another girl asked me if she looked that desperate to me. She was on her way to a pep rally when I asked her to the dance after the game." He looked at Angie's outfit. "Same clothes, different colors, that's all. You're all alike."

And even though Mary Ellen, remembering the picture in the yearbook and feeling very guilty, knew perfectly well that she would have had her fingernails pulled out one by one before she'd have been seen in public with someone who looked like that, she said, "We're not all alike! No one in this room would have treated you like that."

"Maybe not," he admitted, his voice losing life. "You might have used the old 'I've got to wash my hair tonight' excuse, or been overloaded with homework, or had choir rehearsal, or play practice, or cheerleading practice. But the answer would have been no. It was *always* no."

His eyes glittered suspiciously, as if he was holding back tears.

"I tried every diet there ever was," he said, "and I nearly killed myself working out before

I finally got the message that I was wasting my time. I didn't exist for any of you. And I never would."

Before they could say anything, he stood up very straight and said in a brittle voice, "But I existed for you, didn't I, Angie? As long as I had something you wanted, I existed. For once in my life, I was something to a cheerleader. And for a while, I actually had a cheerleader all to myself."

Angie felt as if she was in the middle of a bad dream. She shook her head, blinking rapidly. Her face was ashen, her hands shaking.

"Tell me something," Mary Ellen said crisply. "Did you even put any film in that camera?"

Billy nodded. "Sure. What the heck, I figured carrying pictures of a big-deal cheerleader around with me couldn't hurt. I could always whip them out of my wallet when I needed to impress somebody."

Angie groaned.

Olivia walked over to put an arm around her. "It's okay," she said sympathetically. "It's not your fault. You didn't know. None of us did."

Angie covered her face with her hands.

"You know, we could have you arrested for fraud," Mary Ellen told Billy.

He laughed. "What are you going to use for proof? She didn't sign any contract. She never even asked me for one."

When that sank in, Mary Ellen turned to the others and said in disgust, "Let's get out of here."

But as she and Nancy moved toward the door,

Angie took her hands away from her face, took a deep breath and let it out, and said to Billy with great dignity, "I would like my money back, please."

He shrugged and reached into his pocket. "You can have what's left, after I bought the lights and film." He looked at her with a half grin. "I *did* buy lights and film," he said.

She took the money he handed her. "And if you don't promise me right here and now," she said clearly, "that you won't do this to some other girl, I'm going to go straight to Garrison and tell your aunt and your boss and anyone else who will listen that you're a sleaze and a cheat."

"No sweat," Billy answered with another shrug. "I got what I wanted. No need to repeat."

Angie looked at him. "You know, I think you should get some kind of help. Talk to someone about what you feel, before you really hurt someone — or you get hurt."

Billy Slocum looked away. "Do you care? Whether I get hurt or not?"

Angie thought for a moment. "Sure. Sure I do."

Billy looked at Angie directly. "Maybe I will. Get some help, I mean."

Angie seemed satisfied with that and, giving him one last look, they all left. Olivia was the last one out of the room.

She slammed the door. Hard.

CHAPTER

16

Angie cried all the way to her house. Olivia, sitting next to her in the backseat, tried to comfort her, but it was no use.

"Stupid, stupid, stupid!" she sobbed, her hands covering her face. "Dumb, dumb, dumb!"

They all knew the confrontation in the motel room had dealt a terrible blow to her already shaky self-esteem. They could only hope it wasn't a fatal blow. Angie had to return to her old cheerful, contented self. She *had* to!

But none of them knew the right words to make that happen.

When they reached the Poletti house, she jumped out of the car without a word and ran into the house.

"She shouldn't be alone," Nancy said. "We should stay with her."

"No," Olivia disagreed. "I know how she feels. I've been there. The night I drank too much at Walt's party and made a total fool of myself, I felt like the dumbest creature that ever set foot on this planet. And I hated the thought of facing people. I hated that most of all. She needs to be alone for a little while. We can come over later."

"She's right," Mary Ellen told Nancy, "and I've got to get to work. Could you drop me at the mall?"

They made plans to meet at Angie's that night, with or without an invitation.

"She needs some time to cry it all out," Olivia added on the way to the mall. "But after that, she should be with friends. I just wish I didn't feel so guilty. Like it's *our* fault she's upset. Maybe we should just have minded our own business."

"No," Mary Ellen said firmly. "So she's upset right now. What we have to concentrate on is how she would have felt if it had gone on and on and then the magazine cover never happened." She swiveled on the front seat to look back at Olivia. "I think we should be proud of ourselves. Maybe what we did is making her feel bad right now. But it's saving her a really bad time later on."

Nancy agreed. "I think," she said lightly as she pulled into the mall parking lot, "that we should be very proud of our detective work!"

"Right!" Mary Ellen said. "Especially since we

did it by ourselves! We didn't need the guys to help in any way."

Nancy parked the car. "What I want to know," she said with a wicked glint in her eyes, "is, Are we going to tell the guys 'I told you so' or not?"

"Why, Nancy," Mary Ellen said innocently as she got out of the car, "how could you even think such a thing? What a nasty thought!"

Nancy grinned. "That means yes, right?"

"That means yes," Mary Ellen said. Then she stuck her head in the window and added seriously, "But you could say it to me, too. Because I thought he was the real thing, too."

"So did I," Olivia said.

"Yeah," Nancy said generously. "I guess being cynical, paranoid, and suspicious like me does have its advantages sometimes."

Mary Ellen laughed. "See you at Angie's at eight or so. Are we going to call her first and see if it's okay to come over?"

"No," Olivia decided. "She'll just tell us to leave her alone. I think we should just show up. She won't throw us out."

Nancy and Mary Ellen nodded. "And," Olivia added, "I think we should get the guys over there, too. It might help things seem more normal. I'll call Walt and Pres. You guys can call Ben and Patrick."

Mary Ellen, changing into a plaid wool skirt and silk blouse at Marnie's, wasn't at all sure Patrick would want to see her. And she didn't blame him for being upset with her. Without actually coming right out and *saying* she was going to stay in Tarenton after graduation, she'd certainly given him that impression. Now, with Reese not really Reese, her own hopes about a modeling career had returned, and she couldn't just swallow them whole and make them go away.

But where did that leave Patrick?

Right where he was before, she thought sadly, and maybe this time he won't settle for that.

"I'll come if you think it will help Angie," he said stiffly when she called during her break.

"Oh, I do!" she said, anxious to see him. "She's really down, Patrick. And you mean a lot to her, really." After a minute, she added quietly, "And to me, too. You mean a lot to me, too, Patrick."

"Sure. See you tonight."

She had her work cut out for her. Cheering Angie up wasn't going to be easy, and making Patrick understand why she just couldn't give up her dreams was going to be worse than trying to get a tan in the middle of a blizzard.

The other cheerleaders would help with Angie. After all, her mood affected the entire squad.

But she was on her own with Patrick.

Frowning, she resumed her place on the platform, willing the hours to hurry by so she could straighten out her life.

Four hours later, as they all gathered in front of the Poletti house, she warned, "Now listen, don't anybody bring up that creep's name, okay? We're here to cheer her up, not remind her of him!"

No one argued, and she rang the doorbell.

The girl who answered the ring was a sorry sight. Still in her uniform, the skirt badly wrinkled now, she peered out at them from red and swollen eyes.

"Oh, I get it!" she said instead of her usual, Hi, guys. "This is the therapy session, right? Good friends gathering around the bereaved, to mourn the loss of her pride."

Her voice had a harshness in it that they weren't used to. In the awkward silence that followed, Patrick cleared his throat and stepped forward. "Right!" he said, entering the house before she could stop him. "That's exactly what this is. Only," he added, gesturing with his hand for the others to follow him, "you haven't lost your pride. You've just temporarily misplaced it."

They all followed him inside. Angie pushed her disheveled hair away from her cheeks, keeping her eyes on Patrick.

"And," he added, looking straight at Mary Ellen, "I know what that feels like, believe me."

Mary Ellen flushed and stared at the floor.

"And tell me, doctor," Angie said, folding her arms over her chest and leaning against the front door, "what do you recommend as a cure for this condition?" Even to her own ears, her voice sounded strained. But she couldn't help it.

163

"Nothing," Patrick said flatly.

"Oh, great! Should I just take two aspirin and call you in the morning?"

"You can," Patrick said, removing his jacket and draping it over a potted plant in the hall, "but it won't help. Now, could I please go sit down somewhere? I've had a hard day and I'm beat."

"Well, you might as well," Angie said crankily, moving away from the door. "You sure aren't much help to *me*!"

Silently, she led them all into the long, narrow kitchen. No one seemed sure of just how to behave or what to say. Keeping Reese's name out of the conversation was proving difficult. What else *was* there right now?

Nancy sat on Ben's lap on a kitchen chair, his arms around her waist. Walt and Olivia sat in chairs on opposite sides of the table; Pres leaned against the counter watching Angie pour drinks; and Mary Ellen stood behind Patrick's chair, not touching him.

When the drinks were on the table, Angie stood leaning against the stove, looking at the group seated around the table. They sipped silently, each of them trying desperately to think of the best way to fix things.

"So," Angie said suddenly, looking at Patrick, "you think *you* had a bad day. Wait 'till I tell you about mine!"

And as Mary Ellen, Nancy, and Olivia watched

with wide eyes, Angie related, shakily but honestly, everything that had happened.

When she had finished, as the boys began calling Billy nasty names and sympathizing with Angie, Mary Ellen laughed.

They all stopped talking and stared at her.

"Mind telling us what's so funny?" Angie asked with a disgusted look. "Are you laughing at me?"

"Of course not," Mary Ellen said, still laughing. "I'm laughing at us! We were so careful not to mention Billy's name. And then you jump right in and spill the whole story!" Sobering, she added, "I couldn't have done it, Angie. I know I would have faked it, tried to pretend nothing had happened. I've really got to hand it to you! You're too honest to put on an act.

"And," she continued as Angie's cheeks deepened in color, "if being open and honest like that is what made you trust Billy, I hope that what he did to you doesn't change that about you. Because it really makes you very special."

"Hear, hear!" Pres called from his corner, and the others followed suit by applauding.

Angie came over and sat at the table with them.

"I just feel so dumb," she said, regret in her voice, and then added hastily, "and don't tell me I'm not, because I won't believe you."

Nancy grinned. "I wasn't going to," she said, looking into Ben's eyes. "Were you, Ben?"

Ben shook his head, saying seriously, "Nope, not me. I wasn't going to. Were you, Pres?"

"Not me," Pres said, always willing to go along with a joke. "How about you, Walt?"

They went around the table, each of them shaking a head and saying somberly, "Not me, nope, not me."

It took a few minutes, but Angie finally couldn't stand it another second. The lines of tension faded from her face and she sank back in her chair, the very faintest trace of a smile tugging at her full lips.

"You're all totally rotten," she said, refusing to let the smile escape.

"She's right," Ben said. "We are. Aren't we?"

And they went through the routine again, each of them nodding and saying, "Yep. Yep, we are."

Angie groaned and covered her face with her hands.

"She's laughing," Mary Ellen announced with a triumphant grin. "I can tell."

She put her hands on Patrick's shoulders. He looked up in surprise. At first, he refused to smile. But, seeing her own smile, seeing the old Mary Ellen happy with her co-cheerleaders (and *him*, he had to admit), he found it impossible to stay angry with her.

Besides, he told himself, smiling up at her and reaching up to cover her hands on his shoulders with his hands, Mary Ellen without some kind of dream just wouldn't be Mary Ellen. I think, he told himself, leaning back against her, she'd probably bore me to death.

Someday, he'd figure out a compromise so they could each have what they wanted.

But for right now, maybe it was enough that she was with him. And glad to be, judging by the smile that beamed down on him from her beautiful face.

"I'm *not* laughing!" Angie protested, coming out from behind her hands.

But she had been laughing and they all knew it. There were still tiny little creases at the corners of her mouth, from a grin not yet totally dead.

"Listen," she said seriously, leaning forward, "you don't think he'll go on doing this kind of thing, do you? I mean, I don't see any point in reporting him to the police because I could never prove anything."

"I don't think he'll do it again," Mary Ellen said, leaning down so that her chin was on Patrick's shoulder. "He wanted to get even with us, and he did."

"*I* think," Olivia said, looking across the table at Walt, "that he had a crush on one of those cheerleaders he talked about. And she must have treated him like something you kill with bug spray."

Angie stuck out her chin defiantly. "I know you're all going to yell at me, but I feel sorry for him."

No one yelled at her.

Encouraged by that, she continued. "I've been thinking about the things he said ever since I got home."

"And?" Mary Ellen prompted as Angie paused.

"I think maybe he had a point." She glanced at Olivia, then at Mary Ellen and Nancy. "You saw his picture. You read that his only activity in high school was that one club. I don't think he had any friends at all. Would any of *us* have paid any attention to him?"

The answer, although unspoken, was a resounding no, and they all knew it.

"Well, I don't know about the rest of you," Angie finished, "but I'm going to pay more attention now when I walk through the halls at school and see people I don't know."

"Me, too," Walt said. "The guy was weird, but maybe he had a point."

Olivia and Nancy nodded agreement.

Mary Ellen, leaning on Patrick, said, "Well, I'm *always* friendly. Everybody knows I'm not conceited just because I'm a cheerleader."

There was a long silence.

"C'mon, you guys!" she cried, slapping the table with her hand. "You *know* I'm not conceited!"

Nancy looked at Ben. "Do we know she's not conceited?"

"Sure. Sure, we do," he said with a grin.

"Sure," Pres said, "we know that, don't we, Walt?"

Walt nodded, grinning, and the round robin of nods and grins and, "Sure, you bet's" began.

Suddenly, they were all silent at the same moment. They looked around the room at each other and each one smiled. Once more they had survived something that could have broken them up. Once more they were a team . . . winners . . . but for how long?

Is Pres finally, really, in love? Read Cheerleaders #13, HURTING.

Join the Team!

They're talented. They're fabulous-looking. They're winners! And they've got what you want! Don't miss any of these exciting CHEERLEADERS books!

Books chosen with you in mind from

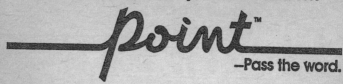

point

—Pass the word.

Living...loving...growing.
That's what **POINT** books are all about!
They're books you'll love reading and
will want to tell your friends about.

Don't miss these other exciting Point titles!

NEW POINT TITLES! $2.25 each